THROUGH MARY'S EYES

Eileen,

May God Bless

You,

Clara Prito

THROUGH MARY'S EYES

Claire A. Patterson M. Ed.

WestBow
PRESS
A DIVISION OF THOMAS NELSON

The St. Joseph Edition of The New American Bible, was used as a reference for some of the passages.

WestBow Press books may be ordered through booksellers or by contacting:

WestBow Press
A Division of Thomas Nelson
1663 Liberty Drive
Bloomington, IN 47403
www.westbowpress.com
1-(866) 928-1240

Because of the dynamic nature of the Internet, any web addresses or links contained in this book may have changed since publication and may no longer be valid. The views expressed in this work are solely those of the author and do not necessarily reflect the views of the publisher, and the publisher hereby disclaims any responsibility for them.

Any people depicted in stock imagery provided by Thinkstock are models, and such images are being used for illustrative purposes only.

Certain stock imagery © Thinkstock.

ISBN: 978-1-4497-2172-5 (e)
ISBN: 978-1-4497-2173-2 (sc)
ISBN: 978-1-4497-2174-9 (hc)

Library of Congress Control Number: 2011912788

Printed in the United States of America

WestBow Press rev. date: 8/12/2011

To my parents, Ruth Flaherty Lachtrupp and Lloyd
Lachtrupp, who always believed in me.
To the Blessed Virgin Mary who loves me with
a love that surpasses all understanding.

Bring all of your joys and sorrows, all of your hopes and despair, all that you are and lay it down at the feet of Jesus. Surrender all to Him! He is your greatest friend and advocate. Only He can stand before the throne of the Father and plead for you. His blood was shed so that He could obtain that purpose and privilege. But never forget our Blessed Mother who loves us with a love that surpasses all understanding. She gathers us beneath her mantle if we only ask. She can protect us from the snares of Satan. Never forget her. Never cease praying.

CONTENTS

PREFACE

I am a cradle Catholic, and Duke (Calvin), my husband, was raised a Seventh - day Adventist. Growing up, I believed in the apparitions of Mary; he did not.

In July 2001, my husband and I traveled to Medjugorje in Bosnia-Herzegovina, where the Blessed Virgin continues to appear daily to certain visionaries. He went reluctantly and only "to protect me from snipers" in a hostile country. He expected to encounter primitive lodging and bad food—certainly nothing miraculous.

Duke was touched by our Blessed Mother, far beyond anything I could have hoped or imagined. Among the many gifts she has given him are glimpses★ into her life. Some lasted only seconds, such as the glimpse of Joseph lying outside the inn with a scraped elbow. Others lasted much longer, e.g., the time Jesus was taken down from the cross and washed by the women.

I took these glimpses and wove them together into the story you are about to read.

Call it fiction if you like, but I hope you will come to know and love the people in these stories as I do. They were real people who walked this earth. They experienced pain, joy, grief, hunger, temptation, betrayal, and love ... lots of love.

Mary holds a unique place in salvation history; she is the beloved Daughter of the Father, the Spouse of the Holy Spirit, and the Mother of Jesus Christ.

The Holy Trinity and the Blessed Virgin Mary are *real* and present in our lives today. They love each of us with a love that surpasses all understanding. They are opening their arms to us and inviting us to love them in return.

Mary has said, "If you only knew how much I love you, you would weep for joy."

My hope is that this book helps you find a loving relationship with Our Lord and His Blessed Mother, and having found it, you weep for joy.

*For more information regarding the glimpses and messages, go to *www.allwhowilllisten.com.*

**Author's note. In chapter 5, a woman named Seraphia wipes Jesus' face with her veil. Tradition holds that her name was Veronica, meaning "true image."

ACKNOWLEDGMENTS

First I want to thank the Father, Son, and Holy Spirit for their many blessings and gifts to our family.

Next I want to thank our Blessed Mother for her ever-present love and guidance.

I want to thank my husband, Duke, for sharing his glimpses, messages, and life with me.

I want to thank my rosary group for their support and suggestions regarding this book. I want to especially thank Joe Gehring and Mary Ann Brausch for their faithful editing of each chapter, and Sally Cox for the title suggestion and encouragement.

I want to thank Michael Brocker of msquaredmedia.com and Nichole Reed for the artwork.

CHAPTER ONE

FINDING LUKE

The old woman looked into the water jar for the third time that morning and sighed. There was no avoiding it. She would have to go for water herself or become too weak to do anything. It had been a long time since she had taken the walk to the well to fetch her own water. She was not looking forward to the strenuous chore. John or Luke or *someone* had always been around to go to the well for her. But now the little band of men and women, who had been her extended family for the past several years, was scattering. Some of them were dead, some were in prison, some were in hiding, and some were traveling. She found herself alone for the first time in fifteen years.

When John had left this time, he'd told her he would be back in two days. He had already been gone for four, and the water jug had been dry since yesterday afternoon. The last bit of bread and fruit had been consumed before that. Luke usually stopped by once or twice a day when John was gone, but he was nowhere to be found. None of the others had come by to visit, which was unusual.

"Where could they all be?" she said aloud as she looked out her door and down the narrow road that led to the valley below. She sighed again, wrapped her mantle about her head and shoulders, and lifted the heavy jug. It took some time to balance the jug on her head. She thought of how she used to swing it up in one motion, balance it there with one hand, and hold her son's tiny hand with the other. Now she felt unsure of her strength. This task that used to be automatic was now difficult. "The well is only a twenty-minute walk away," she tried to reassure herself. "Don't make such a fuss."

It was the beginning of August, and the sun was already baking the earth. As she stepped out from the stone hut, the heat engulfed her like a hot blanket, and she found it difficult to breathe the thick, humid air. The woman looked longingly back at the shade of the cool hut but turned resolutely in the direction of the well. She began walking slowly under the weight of the jug. The path was steep and rocky, and she slowly picked her way down the hill, taking careful aim with each step. She knew that her bones were brittle now, like a small bird's. If she fell, she could easily break a hip or a leg. She might lie helpless for a long time before anyone came by. Her hut sat on a lonely hillside outside the small village of Ephesus. Not many people passed by this way. Most days, it was quiet, with only the birds and small animals to keep her company.

Ten minutes into her walk, she was thirstier than she had been in many years, and the empty water jug seemed heavier with each step. Her mind began racing, and she wondered, "How am I ever going to manage the trip back with a jug full of water? I'm having trouble carrying this *empty* jug! "

At last she found herself at the foot of the hill and at the edge of the town. She turned left to walk down the main street toward the well. There was a row of houses on either side, and she glanced around, looking for a friendly face. She saw several people walking toward her, and there were a few sitting on the ground watching her struggle under her burden. But no one looked on her with compassion. No one seemed to have the time or the inclination to offer help. A few people impatiently brushed past her. Most people acted as if she wasn't even there.

The huts to her left were built right up against the side of the mountain. Some used caves as extra rooms for their homes. The huts to her right were built from stones and handmade bricks and were not as large. Behind them were fields of wild flowers and crops: barley, wheat, and other grains. Most of the plots were small. Olive, lemon, and fig trees separated the row of houses on the right. The little village hummed with activity, and children darted all around.

Watching a young boy run to the well and take a large dipper of water, she thought of her own son when he was that age. Then she remembered a day fifteen years ago when her son was thirsty and carried a heavy burden. The memory brought tears to her eyes, but it also brought a new determination to make it to the well. After all, he had made it up a steep hill with a much heavier burden and in a much more weakened condition. She said a silent prayer, thanking God for the gift of her son, and then added a quick prayer for strength to make it to the well. It seemed so far away!

A little farther down the road, she walked past a familiar doorway. The family there had never been kind to her, but she hoped that perhaps today they would take pity on her and help. A young woman about twenty years of age poked her head out of the door. She was dressed in a gray robe with a dark veil covering her dirty hair. She called back into the house in a mocking tone, "Come out here and see who is getting her own water! The *queen* has finally lost her servants and has to fetch water for herself."

An older man and woman filled the doorway as the younger woman stepped out into the road. They were both strongly built with black-and-silver hair pulled away from their faces with twine. They were covered with gray dust from their pottery-making. They both wore tired expressions, and their bodies sagged from years of heavy labor. They stared at the older woman shuffling under the weight of the jug, then shrugged and returned to the cool shade of their hut.

The young woman continued to stand in the road with her hands on her hips. She did not make any move to help; but as she gazed at the woman's feet sliding in the dust, an old memory came back to her. *Many years ago, when she was a small child, she stood in a doorway much like this one and watched a bloody man walk painfully under the weight of a huge cross. As he passed, she kept her eyes focused on his legs and feet. She remembered them clearly. His robe had been torn in several places, exposing legs that dripped with blood. Then she had focused on his bare feet, covered with dust and blood as her father grabbed her arm, whisked her into the house, and closed the door.*

That was all she'd seen, but the scene played over and over in her nightmares. The memory haunted her to this day. Now she watched this woman's feet. There was something in the movement of those feet that reminded her of the man's feet in her dreams. She turned quickly and went into the house, covering the opening with a leather flap.

The old woman said a quick prayer for the unhappy family and continued walking slowly under the weight of the jug that seemed to increase with each step. The sun burned her eyes, and her head ached from the strain of the task. Five minutes later, she began to stumble and could no longer carry the water jug. She let it down suddenly, nearly breaking it, and then she collapsed in a heap about five hundred paces from the well. She sat in the dusty road and wondered again why she had ever thought she could manage this task. She could never carry the jug full of water back to her hut, even after she had rested and had some water. "Why did I think I could do this?" she croaked to herself. Her own voice startled her. Her tongue felt thick and tasted like the sand that swirled around her. She could not form enough saliva to swallow. She recalled the stories of Moses and the Israelites lost in the desert for forty years. She wished she could strike one of the rocks beside her and find water as Moses had done. But she knew that was a silly wish. This was not a time for miracles. Now she only wanted to make it to the well for a drink of cool water.

She managed to get back to her feet, staggered a few steps, and stumbled over a rock. She tried to block her fall and cut her hand on a sharp rock. She landed hard on one knee, and blood began oozing through her gown before she even felt the sting of the abrasion. She tried to rise again, felt dizzy, and pitched forward, hitting her head on the edge of another rock. Blood began to trickle into her left eye. Her head was pounding and her hands began shaking. She lay in the middle of the road trying to gather her wits. She raised her head up on one elbow and managed to wipe the blood out of her eye with the corner of her veil. As she lay dazed, a woman named Abigail came by with her young daughter Ruth. They were both barefoot and poorly dressed. The little girl, perhaps five years old, had dirty hair pulled back with a strap of leather. Abigail was in her twenties but appeared much older. Her parents and grandparents had once lived in Nazareth and had known the old woman and her family. Abigail's grandfather had been among those who wanted to stone her for carrying a child out of wedlock. Abigail's family had fled to Ephesus twenty years ago to escape the Roman taxes and persecutions. As she looked at the lady in the street, Abigail remarked cruelly, "Look at that old woman, Ruth. Look what she's come to, lying in the dust." Then she leaned down, waved her finger near the old woman's face, and lectured, "This is what happens when you have relations with a man before marriage."

Then she turned back to her daughter and said, "Yahweh is punishing her, Ruth, for her sins of many years ago." Abigail walked a few steps further and said quietly to herself, "Her sins must have been great in God's eyes, for all she has suffered."

The little girl ignored her mother's harsh words and ran to put her arm on the old woman's shoulder. "Can I help? Can I get you some water?" she offered.

Ruth had always liked this kind, old woman with the warm, blue eyes and friendly smile. Her mother never wanted her to go near the old woman's hut, but Ruth had never understood why. All she knew was that this woman had been kinder to her than anyone else in her short life.

Ruth had visited the old woman several times when her mother was too busy or too tired to notice she was gone. She would walk up the steep path to the cool hut on the side of the mountain. She was always welcomed with a warm smile and a bit of fruit or bread.

Often they talked about a wonderful place called heaven as they shared a small meal and watched the animals nearby. The old woman would tell Ruth about her son who had died long ago.

Ruth's favorite story was about the time her son had scolded others for keeping children away from him. She loved to hear the old woman talk about how her son gathered the children into his arms and danced and sang songs with them. She said that he loved to play with children, and his laughter was the most wonderful sound in the world.

Sometimes the old woman would teach Ruth songs she had sung with her son when he was a small boy. The woman's voice was the sweetest sound Ruth had ever heard.

Now, on this hot dusty road, the old woman looked so tired and thirsty. Sweat was streaming down her face and dampening her hair. Her hand and head were bleeding and caked with dirt. The old woman looked up with her beautiful eyes, smiled, and nodded. Ruth could barely hear her scratchy voice as she answered, "Yes, thank you, dear. A drink of water would be wonderful."

The girl's mother jerked the tiny arm away and pulled her to the other side of the road. "We are not going to help that old woman, Ruth. Move along." The girl looked back sadly and waved secretly as the woman gave her a kind smile.

A few minutes later, as the girl and her mother came back from the well and passed by her, the little girl sprinkled some cool water on the old woman's head, almost in blessing. Her reward was another beautiful smile and a true blessing in return.

The woman tried to rise again but could not. She used the last of her energy to scoot herself to the side of the road. When she felt safely out of the way of passing animals and carts, she rested her head on her arm. The sun felt like an oven when the door opens suddenly to take out baking bread. She had a quick thought that perhaps she should try to sit up, and then she lost consciousness.

Sometime later, she felt someone gently moving her shoulder to turn her over. As her head rolled toward the light, she fell back again. She heard a frantic voice that seemed far away: "Mother Mary, my precious mother! Are you all right? What has happened?"

Mary stirred, still groggy, and tried to open her eyes, but the light was too bright. She recognized his voice before she could see him.

It was Luke. He had finally returned to Ephesus. Mary couldn't speak. Her throat was too dry, and she began shaking with the effort to rise. Luke said, "Don't move, Mother. I'm here now. I will take care of you." Then he tenderly gathered her into his arms. He carried her to the shade of a nearby house.

She seemed so light. It was like carrying a child. He was afraid she hadn't been eating much lately. "Mother, have you been fasting again?" he asked as he carried her across the road.

Mary had told Luke many times, and anyone else who would listen, that fasting always helped make prayer more efficacious. And, like a good mother, she taught more with example than with words.

He sat her up against the wall of the nearest house and put his arm around her shoulder. They were in the shade now, but the heat was still intense.

She opened her eyes and struggled to focus. He gazed into her eyes. They were still so beautiful. They were the color of the little wildflowers growing in the field behind them. He had never seen eyes that color on anyone else.

But her real beauty came from the love she projected. Her gaze penetrated him. He always felt that she could read his soul. When he was a young boy, she had been able to look into his eyes and know what kind of a day it had been for him. If he had been selfish, her eyes reflected disappointment. If he had been praying faithfully or treating others kindly, her eyes sparkled with joy.

Sometimes Luke envied the others who had known her longer, especially John.

John and Mary seemed to have a unique relationship. But Luke and Mary had their special times alone, and he treasured them like precious jewels in a box buried in a sacred place. He had stored them in his memory so that at any time in his life he could examine them one by one and recall each detail.

Now, as he held her, Luke noticed her hair had come undone and was peeking out from under her veil. Pieces of hair were clinging to her shrunken cheeks. Her hair was almost completely white now, but there were still a few strands of the black, wavy hair from her youth. He wished he had known her when she was young. How beautiful she must have been! Now her eyes were surrounded by dark shadows and deep lines. Her skin was brittle and dry after so many years of living in harsh, dry climates.

"Mother, do you think you can sit here by yourself? I need to go and get water from the well."

She nodded weakly and braced herself with her good hand against the smooth stone by the wall. Then Luke raced the short distance to the well, his tunic flying like a curtain blowing in the wind.

Even though he had been walking all morning in the hot sun, Luke felt a surge of renewed energy. He was twenty-six years old—strong, healthy, and sinewy. He had gentle features and curly brown hair streaked with blond from days of walking in the sun. His eyes were dark and penetrating, and they displayed wisdom beyond his years.

As Mary watched Luke run to the well, she remembered the first time she had seen him.

He was only eleven years old then but looked more like eight or nine. He was very thin with sad eyes. He wore a band of iron on his left arm and another on his right ankle. These bands branded him as a slave. He stood behind a column a few feet from Pilate as Jesus tottered on the platform before the crowd. The little boy tried to be inconspicuous and clearly did not want to be near the scene of such cruelty, but he seemed to be looking at Jesus, mesmerized.

As pilot address the people below, the little boy looked out into the crowd. His eyes locked on Mary's. Somehow this little boy knew Jesus was her son. He gazed on her with compassion.

Jesus had been scourged thirty-nine times and was bleeding from all parts of his body. The Roman whips had three leather straps with pieces of sharp metal at each end. They were cruel instruments of torture. He also wore a crown meant to mock him, woven from thorn branches. This caused blood to stream down his face, making it difficult for him to see. One of his eyes was swollen shut from the beatings, and the other was blinking erratically, trying to keep the blood at bay. There were deep cuts in his cheeks where the crown had slipped and then been forced back up over his face and back onto his head. One of the thorns was piercing an ear and the other was dangerously close to his one good eye.

His arms were tied behind his back, making it difficult for him to keep his balance. Suddenly, he tipped to one side and fell against a soldier. The soldier acted like he had just been touched by a leper and pushed Jesus away.

The crowd roared with laughter as other soldiers joined in the pantomime and pushed Jesus back and forth, all pretending to brush the touch of a leper off of their bodies. Finally Pilate lost patience and demanded that everyone stand still.

Mary looked back at Luke. This little boy was the only one near Jesus who did not look at her son with scorn. He seemed to want to reach out to help Jesus, but clung to the column instead, half-hidden in shame.

Then suddenly the crowd was crying, "Crucify him! Crucify him!" and Mary was overcome with sadness. She covered her eyes with her hands and leaned against John as his strong arm supported her. When she glanced up again, she saw a soldier jerk on the rope around Jesus' waist to move him down the steps and across the citadel yard. Her son stumbled and almost fell, but there were so many soldiers surrounding him, he was held up by the crush of their bodies. Suddenly, the crowd began moving like a giant, rolling wave to follow the sad parade.

Mary was in shock and couldn't move her feet. As John and Mary Magdalene tried to urge her forward, she was knocked to the ground. People began stumbling over her in their rush to see the torture continue. When John was able to get her to her feet, the platform was empty and the crowd was thinning. Just then, the little slave boy appeared. He had a wet cloth and some salve. He spoke gently to her in a language she did not understand, as he carefully examined her for injuries. He applied some cream to a few cuts as Mary gently pushed him away and whispered, "We must go." John quickly thanked the little boy, and off they rushed to follow the crowd and find Jesus.

As Mary lay on the ground watching Luke draw water from the well, she said a quick prayer of thanksgiving for this wonderful man. She remembered the stories he had told her long ago, when they first began to know one another.

When he was only six years old, his educated and well-to-do parents sent him from their plantation home in Greece to the nearby city of Antioch. He was to serve as an apprentice with a physician in the large city. This physician noticed Luke's intelligence and special talents and introduced him to several of his friends. One of them, a renowned artist of the time, took a special liking to Luke. When the physician released him for a few hours each day, Luke would run to the artist's home and learn sketching and painting from him. Luke's quest for knowledge was never-ending.

When Luke was nine, the Romans invaded Antioch. They killed the physician, the artist, and everyone who was either too old or too young to serve their army. They kept Luke alive to act as a slave to the foot soldiers. He was forced to serve the men their meals and carry their water. He was small and very thin and becoming weaker with each day. If he dropped anything or was too slow, the soldiers would beat him. Pilate noticed this small boy with unusual intelligence, struggling to survive. He was different from the other young boys captured in Antioch. Pilate was afraid that the little boy would not live long under the cruelty of the soldiers, so he decided to claim Luke as his personal slave.

Soon they all boarded a ship and sailed to different ports all through the Mediterranean Sea, taking on supplies and exchanging soldiers and slaves. Pilate gave Luke free reign of the ship, and he soon regained his old confidence and thirst for knowledge. He learned Geography from the ship's officers. He learned more about healing from the ship's doctor, and he learned about food preparation from the ship's galley chef.

Two months later, they arrived in a place called Caesarea. Pilate led Luke off and took him to a palace by the shore. This palace had been built by Herod and was very grand. Luke had never seen such wealth. Pilate brought Luke into his wife's chambers and told him to do whatever Claudia or her maids asked of him. Luke bowed low and sat in a corner waiting for the lady to arrive. One of her maids came in and told Luke to stay quiet and out of the way because their mistress was having one of her bad headaches. Then she rushed off as they heard footsteps approaching the chamber. It was Claudia. She was a lovely lady wearing fine flowing gowns. Her hair had been pulled up behind her neck and she wore bracelets of gold. Luke watched as she groaned and lay upon the bed, not even noticing the small boy cowering in the corner.

When the lady left, the maid came in with a tray of food for Luke. He was ravenous and devoured every crumb. She told him to sleep on the pallet by the window and just do as he was told. Luke spent several days just listening to the sounds of the house and looking longingly out the window. The sea was so beautiful. The colors of the water were blue and green and *many shades in between. He wanted so much to be outside running on the beach or in the fields beyond the palace.*

One day, as Claudia groaned from the pain of another headache, Luke meekly suggested that he might be able to help. He asked for permission to go out into the garden beneath the window and into the field beyond to gather herbs. Claudia agreed and called for her maid to go with him. She thought he was an odd sort of servant: always quiet and with a special light in his eye.

He returned a short time later with a cool drink for Claudia. He told her to sip it slowly as he wrapped soft rags around the back of her neck. The rags had been dipped in something sweet-smelling, and the fragrance soothed her. Then he gently massaged her head, neck, and shoulders. Her headache went away during the treatment. She felt better than she had in months. She told her maid to fix a special meal for Luke and then went out to find her husband to thank him for bringing her such a wonderful slave.

After that day, Claudia kept Luke near. One day he was ordered to follow Claudia to the beach. She wanted to wade in the water, as the heat was oppressive.

Luke sat down in the sand near the water and began sculpting the figure of a man. Claudia, curious, walked by and noticed his talent. When they got back to the palace, she ordered paints and a canvas brought to Luke to see what he could do with that. She had an enjoyable afternoon asking him to paint objects in the room. Then she asked him if he could paint a portrait of her. Luke spent several pleasurable days painting in Claudia's chambers.

One rainy day, Claudia called her husband to her room to see the finished portrait. As Pilate walked over to the painting, Luke noticed that he winced in pain. Pilate said, "Well done," and then patted Luke on the head. "I knew I made a good choice in selecting you as my slave."

As he began to walk out of the room, Luke spoke up bravely. "Sir, I think I can help with the pain in your joints. I just need permission to go outside the palace gate to gather herbs." Pilate, not yet trusting this strange boy, gave permission, but sent a soldier to secretly follow him.

Luke went out into the fields and gathered some seeds and leaves. He came back immediately to the house and concocted a special ointment by crushing the leaves and seeds and then boiling them in water. The soldier reported to Pilate that there had been no attempt to escape and then brought Luke into Pilate's study where he was looking over maps. Luke waited quietly in the corner until summoned. Eventually Pilate waved for Luke to come over and sent the others out of the room. He said, "Now, what do you have there? It reeks. Are you sure it won't make me sick?"

Luke bowed low and said, "No, my lord, it will ease the pain in your joints."

"Get on with it then," Pilate said gruffly as he eased himself gently into a large chair and pulled his tunic up to his thighs.

Luke had small, delicate hands, and as he massaged the ointment into the older man's knees, Pilate began to feel a warm sensation slowly move to his joints. A few minutes later, he felt less pain. He stood up and walked across the room. "This is wonderful, my boy! You need to do this each time the weather becomes rainy or humid, or whenever I am back from riding, or when I am under a lot of stress, or … just whenever I hurt badly." Luke smiled secretly. He knew that as long as he made himself useful to these two powerful people, he might secure a better life. Life was good for Luke by the beautiful sea—at least as good as life could be for a slave who had lost his parents and seen his mentors and friends murdered or captured.

As the weather turned colder, Pontius Pilate received a transfer to Jerusalem. He was not happy about the assignment, but he had no choice. He decided to bring Claudia and Luke with him to make the post more bearable. No one wanted to leave the beautiful palace by the sea to live in a large, walled city, but they had orders and had no choice. A governor, wife, and slave must all do as they were commanded.

Claudia had nightmares for days before the move. She dreamed that the city was full of ghosts and that the streets ran with blood. She begged Pilate not to make her move, but he could not stand the thought of being without her for what could be a year or more.

The winter in Jerusalem was colder than normal, and Pilate and Claudia struggled to make a new life in the city palace. Luke adjusted easily. He soon grew accustomed to the busy life in Jerusalem. Pilate and Claudia trusted him, and he was given freedom to go to the market for herbs for the medicines he made.

The soldiers usually left him alone, but when they did bother with him, it was to ask him to treat their illnesses or injuries. They didn't remember the days they had mistreated this small boy. Of course, Luke never forgot. He never trusted the soldiers, nor did he ever forget their potential for cruelty. He stayed out of their way as much as possible. That spring morning, when Mary had first spotted Luke hiding behind a pillar, Pilate had been in a great deal of pain. He had sent for Luke just as the soldiers were bringing Jesus in.

Earlier that morning Luke had been rubbing Claudia's head and putting cold cloths on her neck, as she was having another one of her terrible headaches. Her nightmares had only intensified since moving to Jerusalem, and she had experienced a terrible one the night before. When the soldier entered the room to collect the boy for Pilate, Claudia instructed Luke to tell her husband about her most recent dream.

When Luke came before Pilate, he saw a man standing nearby with hands bound behind his back. He had been badly beaten, but he stood patiently waiting for Pilate. As Luke massaged Pilate's joints, he delivered Claudia's message. "My lord, your wife told me to tell you that she had a terrible nightmare about this man last night. She said that you should have nothing to do with him. She said he is innocent and has committed no crime." Pilate was beginning to put stock in his wife's dreams and listened carefully. Luke could tell that this message disturbed Pilate. In a dark mood, he told Luke to stay nearby.

Luke hid behind a pillar as he watched Pilate try to find a way to release Jesus. The man became frustrated and then angry as he argued with the Jewish leaders—to no avail.

Luke knew that Jesus was an innocent man. He trusted in Claudia's dreams, but it was more than that; he sensed something very noble and holy in this man. As he watched the prisoner being dragged up the stairs, he wondered again at the cruelty of the Roman soldiers. There was no need to whip him so many times or torment and mock him with a crown of thorns. As Luke stood on the platform that morning, Jesus was only five paces away. As much as he wanted to turn away, he couldn't stop looking at the man. From where he stood, he could see a thorn piercing his skin just above his right eyebrow. His left eye was already swollen shut from earlier beatings.

Jesus had been scourged so many times that blood was soaking his tunic and running down his legs. There was a small pool of blood that gathered at his feet, making him slip and nearly fall. This only made the crowd and the soldiers roar with laughter.

Luke wondered how Jesus was able to remain on his feet. A few weeks before, Luke had heard a soldier brag about killing a man with his whip. They used such cruel instruments for torture! He also wondered at this man's bravery. He never pleaded for mercy as so many others had. In spite of his injuries and the treatment of the soldiers, he looked dignified and at peace. Luke marveled at the prisoner's composure.

At one point, Pilate took Jesus aside and spoke to him privately, but Luke and a few of the soldiers could hear. Pilate asked, "Are you the king of the Jews?" Jesus spoke through his swollen lips very quietly. "You say so." Then Jesus said, "My kingdom does not belong to this world."

Later, Luke heard a frustrated Pilate say to Jesus when he refused to defend himself: "Why do you not speak to me? Do you not know that I have the power to release you, and I have the power to crucify you?"

Luke was astonished to hear Jesus reply in a very strong, clear voice, "You would have no power over me if it had not been given to you from above." This was embarrassing for Pilate, as some of the soldiers heard Jesus' response. Still Pilate did not want to order the death of this innocent man. Desperate for a way out, Pilate tried one more tactic. He turned to the crowd and offered the release of one prisoner—Jesus or the thief and murderer, Barabbas. Luke could not believe his ears as the crowd shouted for the criminal Barabbas to be released. Luke had never seen anything so wrong.

Immediately Pilate ordered Luke to bring him a bowl of fresh water so he could wash his hands in front of the crowd. Pilate did all he could to heed his wife's warnings, but the pressure from the mob below left him no choice.

As Luke looked into the angry crowd, he spotted a woman whose eyes were the most beautiful he had ever seen. Somehow Luke knew she was the innocent man's mother. There was no hate in her eyes for the Romans or the people demanding her son's death. He saw only forgiveness and love. He didn't understand much of what happened that day, but he knew he had to find out more about this quiet man of courage and his gentle mother. Suddenly Jesus was pulled down the steps. Pilate went back inside, and Luke watched as the mob knocked the woman down. He grabbed some of his medicines quickly and ran to help her.

Later that evening, the soldiers talked fearfully about how the sky had become suddenly dark when Jesus was hanging on the cross. They talked about the earthquake that occurred when he died.

When these events happened, Luke heard Claudia plead with her husband to leave Jerusalem as soon as possible. She left that evening in great haste for their palace in Caesarea with only two women and one soldier to accompany her. Pilate sent a messenger to Rome the next morning requesting a transfer to anywhere but Jerusalem.

That same Saturday, Luke heard the soldiers talking about how the condemned man forgave them, even as they were driving the nails into his hands and feet. One of the soldiers had won Jesus' robe in a game of bones and decided he didn't want it. He was afraid that it might have a curse on it. He said it was stained with so much blood, it was useless.

Luke watched the soldier throw the robe into a trash heap and walk away wiping his hands against his leggings. Luke retrieved it later while the soldiers were busy eating. He took it out reverently, washed, dried, and folded it carefully. He hid the precious relic under his sleeping mat that evening. As he drifted off to sleep, he decided to find the man's mother and give it to her. He had no idea how he would do this, but he fell asleep peacefully just thinking about meeting her some day.

When Luke woke up on Sunday, the soldiers were talking about the dead man again. This news was astounding! He had disappeared from his grave. Some said his body had been stolen; others said he was still alive. Others said that his ghost was walking around Jerusalem.

The soldiers who had been assigned to guard his tomb said they had been knocked unconscious by Jesus' followers. They were not around for dinner that evening, and Luke never saw them again. He did not know if the soldiers had been killed, transferred, or put in prison.

Luke thought a lot about the woman with the kind, beautiful eyes. He tried to find out where she lived, but no one at the palace knew anything about her.

Three weeks later, the soldiers were still ill at ease and making Luke's life miserable. With Claudia gone, he had much less protection from their cruelty. They were jealous of the little slave who ate better than they did and slept in the beautiful palace. They said he was treated more like a free child than a cowering slave.

Their nerves were on edge since the man had died and disappeared from his tomb. On top of all of this, they had been ordered to find the missing body and those who had taken it. They searched and searched but could not find anything or anyone connected to the man who had died on the cross. Luke heard some say that they were afraid to find his body or his friends. They worried about curses and powers beyond human strength. So they drank a lot and began taking out their frustrations on weaker, defenseless people around them.

Two of the soldiers, after finishing off a jug of wine, decided to teach little Luke a lesson about Roman masters and slaves. They watched him walk outside the palace gate toward the marketplace. They threw the jug aside and staggered after him. They caught up to him quickly, and the larger one grabbed Luke's thin arm and pulled him close to his face. His breath smelled so strong that it made Luke a bit dizzy. He could feel his arm bruising and wondered what he had done to irk them this time. The solder told him it was time he learned a lesson about how a proper slave should behave. He jerked Luke's little body into the air like a rag doll. Luke, in a panic, kicked hard at the man's genitals. His foot landed on target, and the soldier let his arm go with a wail. The other soldier began laughing as Luke landed running. The small boy made it quickly to the marketplace and dove under a table with a long cloth surrounded by people.

As he peeked up to see where the soldiers were, he saw the woman he had dreamed about many times over the last three weeks. "Please, dear lady, help me," he pleaded quietly. Without a word, she drew him near her and covered him completely with her mantle. At that moment, the two soldiers came to the table and looked beneath it. The soldier who had been kicked pounded his fist onto the table and walked away looking under all of the nearby tables and baskets. The two men made quite a disturbance in the marketplace. Most of the people stopped their activities and just stood in quiet fear, hoping the soldiers would not take out their anger on them. After what seemed like a long time, the men became tired and thirsty, and gave up their search. They decided to head back to the palace for more wine and shuffled back down the dusty road toward the palace.

"It's all right now, little one. You can come out," the woman whispered. Luke came out quickly and kissed her hand. Mary suddenly realized that this was the little slave boy she had met the morning of her son's death. He was still trembling, but he did not want to bring the wrath of the guards upon this dear woman. He kissed her hands one more time and ran in the direction opposite the palace. Eventually he headed back to Claudia's chambers the long way around. One of Claudia's maids brought him food and drink, and he refused to leave the protective chambers for three days.

Four weeks later, Luke was walking past the temple on an errand for Pontius Pilate. He saw several Jewish men shouting in the courtyard. At first he thought they were drunk, but as he listened, he realized that they were just passionate about their words. Then he stopped in amazement; he could understand every word these men were saying. They seemed to be speaking in his native tongue! He hadn't heard his own language spoken in three years! As he looked around, everyone nearby seemed to understand what this man was saying as well. This was very strange, as most people in Jerusalem did not know Luke's native tongue. Then he became enthralled by the words. They talked about Jesus; the man he had seen tortured and sent to his death. Luke felt drawn in. He had to find out more about this man they said was raised from the dead.

Then he saw the man called John who had been with the mother of Jesus of Nazareth that terrible day. He listened and waited until John was about to leave. Luke shyly approached the young apostle.

John looked to be about eighteen years of age, with only the start of a beard. He had kind eyes and was dressed in simple but clean clothing that showed signs of mending. He smelled slightly of fish. Luke trusted him instinctively. He began asking questions in rapid order. "How could everyone understand when you spoke in my native tongue? Where is Jesus now? Where is his kingdom? How is his mother? Who is taking care of her? I have his robe. How can I return it to his mother?"

John remembered this young boy from the morning of the crucifixion. He remembered his kindness toward Mary and believed that this slave to the Romans was sincere.

They were standing in the hot sun, and it seemed as if the questions would go on for a very long time, so John invited Luke back to Mary's rooms. The little boy seemed most anxious to see her, and he seemed heartfelt in his quest to know more about Jesus.

Luke was overjoyed to see Mary again. She was so gentle and loving. He rushed to kneel before her and kissed her hands reverently. "Dear lady, I want to give you a gift. I have your son's robe hidden in the palace. May I come again and return it to you?"

"Yes, my son," she said as she raised him to his feet. "You may come and visit as many times as it is safe for you. I would love to hold my son's robe in my arms once again. I am happy to see you are unharmed. Now go back before you are missed, and I will look forward to your visit another day." Luke left reluctantly but promised he would return soon.

In the days that followed, Luke invented many excuses to leave Pilate's palace. He was a trusted slave, and no one questioned his need to go out to gather herbs and medicines. While running these errands, he spent as much time as he could with John and Mary. When he brought her the robe, cleaned but still stained with Jesus' blood, tears filled her eyes with the memory of his agony. Then she began singing and rejoicing in his resurrection.

John told Luke about Jesus' visits to them after his resurrection. He told Luke about Jesus' ascension into heaven. He explained that they had all been afraid of the Jewish high priests and the Roman soldiers during and after Jesus' death, but since the Holy Spirit had descended like a dove and enlightened them with tongues of fire, they were no longer afraid. Luke felt moved when he heard these accounts. He believed every word John and the others shared with him. He understood that the guards had lied about the corpse being stolen.

Luke wanted the courage and peace these men and women had. He wanted to be part of this amazing family, and he asked to be baptized.

John and Mary baptized Luke in the upper room with a pitcher of water, as slaves were not permitted to leave the walled city to go to the river. At the moment of his baptism, Luke received the Holy Spirit into his heart. He felt like he had a mother and brothers and sisters and he felt the love of his Father in heaven. His heart was burning with love.

Luke wanted to spread the words of Jesus as the others were doing, but the apostles warned him of the dangers he would face if he did. He was still Pilate's slave. He was still very young. He needed to be careful and remain safe until the time was right. Luke also felt called to protect Mary and to care for her. He had seen the agony in her eyes the day her son died, and he wanted to guard her from any more pain.

Four months had passed since the death and resurrection of Jesus, and Pilate's request for transfer had finally been granted. He planned to leave immediately for Caesarea and then move with Claudia to Rome. Luke begged Pilate for his freedom. Pilate did not want to lose his little healer, but Claudia had experienced another disturbing dream. She wrote to her husband that if he took Luke away from Jerusalem, Pilate would become very sick and die from a high fever. She said Luke must be left behind. This time Pilate listened to his wife and believed in her dream. Luke's iron bands were removed. He was no longer a slave and was free to live anywhere he chose.

Pilate let him keep his paints, canvases, mixing bowls, and extra clothing and gave him a bag of food as parting gifts. Luke bowed low before Pilate and turned quickly away from his former life. He exited the palace, running through the back gate to avoid the two guards who were still angry with him.

Luke hadn't seen his parents in six years. Finding them was out of the question. They had probably been killed or sold into slavery at the same time he had been captured by the Romans, so he moved in with Mary and John. Mary was happy to have the young boy around, and Luke soon proved to be helpful. He ministered to the apostles when they returned from jail and scourging. He also delighted the growing faith community with paintings of Mary and the apostles. Luke was a joy to all, but especially to Mary. He could bring a smile to her face when others could not.

Luke felt tightness in his chest as he ran for the water. He had let his adopted mother down. He had left her alone for far too long! He hurried back, tripping on stones and almost spilling the water from the gourd. When he came near her, he slowed his pace so he wouldn't kick dust into her face. He held her gently and let her sip the water slowly. It was the sweetest water Mary had tasted in a long time.

When the dipper was empty, he raced back to the well, this time taking the water jug Mary had brought from home. He needed more water for her to drink and to clean her wounds.

When he returned this time, Luke began to examine Mary carefully. He discovered a deep cut in the palm of her right hand where she had fallen on a sharp stone. She was also bleeding through her gown from her knee, and a cut on her forehead was oozing blood. He opened his pouch and pulled out some strips of cloth and salve that he always brought with him on his travels. He took her hand gently into his and washed the wound. As he cleaned the pebbles and dust from the cut, it began to bleed again. He applied pressure until the bleeding stopped and then wrapped some of the clean strips of cloth tightly around her hand.

He got another clean cloth from his bag and began to wash the blood from her face and knee. He gently rubbed salve on the scraped skin of her knee. As he ministered to her, he lowered his voice so those passing by would not hear. "Where is John? Why did he leave you alone? Why didn't you wait for me to come back?"

Mary tried to speak, but she was having difficulty breathing, and no words would come out. Luke held her tight, gave her another sip, and waited until her breathing became normal. She sighed and said, "Dearest Luke, what would I do without you?"

She gently patted his hand with her good hand and then rested it in his larger one. Her touch always gave him a sense of peace. She had a way of making the darkest hour seem light. She transmitted love with everything she did: her look, her touch, her voice. How he loved this wonderful woman!

CHAPTER TWO

TELL ME A STORY

As Luke cradled his adopted mother Mary in his arms, he looked at their two hands together. The contrast was sharp. His hand was tanned and strong; hers was small, and the skin was almost transparent. Her normal olive complexion had turned pale, and the blue veins on the tops of her hands seemed to pop out with a vulnerability that worried Luke.

"Where is John?" he asked again, this time in exasperation.

Mary whispered between small sips of cool water, "He left four days ago. We got word that Peter had been thrown into prison in Rome. I insisted that John leave immediately to confirm the report and see what could be done. I sent him off with food and a blanket. He said he would be back in two days, but something must have happened to delay him. He thought you were here in Ephesus and that you would be checking in with me each day."

Luke answered, "I *was* here four days ago, but I had to leave to see about Paul. I didn't think to tell anyone. I thought John was with you. I heard Paul was taken prisoner, and I needed to find someone who could tell me where he is. I learned he had been taken to Caesarea. I was just returning to get supplies for the long journey. If I hadn't returned just now, who knows what might have happened? Oh, Mother, what are we going to do? It's getting harder each day. Our little band of brothers and sisters are arrested, beaten, and dying ..." Luke suddenly became quiet and bowed his head. "I get so afraid for all of us sometimes."

Mary just looked into his liquid-brown eyes and smiled. "Dear Luke, you are tired from your journey and probably very hungry. Let's go home and wash up and then, perhaps, you can find something to eat. I can hear your stomach growling like an angry dog. You will feel much better with food and rest." With that, she gave him one of her glorious smiles and squeezed his hand.

He felt better immediately. Her smile could make any worry disappear. Luke wondered what he would have done all these years if he had never met her. And then, as he looked at her thin, pale face, he wondered how he would ever live without her. She was old, he reflected, and very weak. He knew that one day, possibly before the next winter, she would be gone.

Mary was feeling much better after the rest and refreshment. With Luke's strong arm for support, she stood up slowly and spoke in a steady voice, "Well, now, first things first. Let's get the water jug home and wash up, and then you can fetch us a nice lunch. I will help you prepare for your journey to Caesarea. You must go to help Paul as soon as possible."

Luke knew she was right, but he also knew he could not leave her alone. Luke gathered the container of salve and pieces of cloth into his bag and strapped it around his waist. Then he picked up the water jug, balanced it on his head with one arm and hooked his free arm into hers. They walked slowly back to Mary's home, sharing friendly glances with curious onlookers. The hill was a difficult and slow climb for Mary hampered by her swollen knee, but with Luke's strong arm and encouragement, she finally made it.

Mary lived in a one-room stone hut halfway up a rocky hill outside Ephesus. John had built it from materials he found locally. It was cool in the summer and provided good shelter in bad weather. It was small but all she and John needed.

It was rectangular in shape, with a flat roof that could be used for extra living space when desired. There was a sturdy ladder leaning against one side.

The hut was surrounded with pink, purple, red, and white wildflowers, with a small vegetable garden to the south side of the hut. There were two small windows near the top of the building on opposite sides to allow the air to flow freely. In bad weather, there were leather flaps that could be brought down over the windows and fastened from the inside.

Several paces beyond the door was a large fire pit ringed by flat stones. Over the pit was a tall, wooden structure on which hung a metal cauldron. In the middle of the fire pit, John had built a brick oven with an iron door, so Mary could bake her own bread. The iron had been difficult to come by, but he had worked for people in town until he earned enough money to have it made by a local iron-worker.

Inside the hut was a low stool near a short-legged table in the center of the room. There was a large chest in one corner that contained most of Mary's personal belongings. These were the only pieces of furniture in the room. John had constructed a few shelves for the walls, on which Mary stored her meager supply of jugs, bowls, and cups.

There was a basket of sewing supplies on the floor by the stool, and a small wooden box for candles, flints, and odds-and-ends just inside the door. A basket for fruit sat on the low table and a jar for flour rested in a corner of the room. Luke noticed that both of these containers were empty.

There were two mats rolled up and stored alongside one wall. John used one to sleep by the door, and Mary used the other to sleep near the back of the room. She was often cold now, even on summer nights. There were extra blankets rolled up beside her mat.

One wall was lined with tapestries Mary had woven during her life. She used these to keep out the cold winds in the winter and to provide a more comfortable back rest when she sat on the floor.

As Mary slowly hobbled into the hut, she gazed at the chest in the back corner. Mary began thinking back to the first time she had seen it. "Luke, did I ever tell you how I got that chest?"

"No, Mother. Tell me after I build a fire and put some water on for washing." Luke unrolled her mat and eased her onto it near the wall with the tapestries.

Mary winced as she moved her swollen knee. She watched Luke take the flint stones from the box and begin to build a fire outside. When he returned, she spoke steadily.

The chest was a wedding present from Joseph. Now I keep my treasures in it. They are of little worth to others, but precious to me.

When I first saw it, I behaved like a little child. I ran my hands over the smooth surface and tested the lid. It fit straight and tight. Even my father was excited about the gift. He said it was well made, and he slapped Joseph on the back in congratulations.

I nearly lost my chest twice. The first time was only a few months after our marriage. Joseph carried it over to my parents' home before we left for Bethlehem. We all thought we would be back in two weeks.

"I remember the second time, Mother," Luke interjected. "We were on our way here and nearly lost it in the storm crossing the sea."

"Yes, my son. That was a difficult journey, but not as difficult as our trip to Bethlehem and Egypt."

After Jesus was born earlier than expected, we made the trip to Jerusalem for his presentation and circumcision. After that, we had to travel to Egypt and years of exile.

I did not see Nazareth again until four years later. I remember the day we returned to Nazareth with my small son.

My mother had learned from Elizabeth that my baby was born well but that Herod had sent soldiers to kill all of the infant boys in the region not long after Jesus was born. Elizabeth was told that we had fled to safety, but had no knowledge of where we had gone or even if we were still alive.

My mother had faith that our little family was still safe, for she believed that the baby was a great gift from God and would be protected by him. She believed the angel had spoken to me and that my child was the Son of God. She believed the angel had spoken to Joseph to encourage him to take me as his wife. And so, she believed that somehow God would send his angel to protect us from the Roman soldiers.

But until she saw our family walking down the dusty street toward our home, she could never be sure she would ever see us again. What a homecoming that was! My mother nearly fainted with joy, seeing me and her grandson whole and healthy. In her joy, my cousin Salome raced from home to home telling the neighbors of our arrival. Some Nazarenes were happy for us and came to welcome us, but most chose to turn their backs as a sign of their disapproval. In the opinion of many, we had conceived our child before marriage and should be banished.

My father had died the winter before we returned, so the homecoming was bittersweet. We decided to move into my mother's hut, as it was larger than ours, and Joseph and I could help take care of her in her advanced years.

I found my chest in a corner and began to fill it with our things.

Now, after a few moves and many years later, the lid doesn't fit so snugly, and it is not as beautiful as it once was, but it is still precious to me.

Luke gave Mary one more drink of cool water and began checking for supplies. He noticed there was no food in the hut, so he brought out the last bit of cheese and bread he had in his pouch. He gave it to Mary and then went outside with a dipper and bowl to fetch some warm water for washing. He brought this back inside and placed it beside Mary as she chewed the last piece of cheese.

He placed a clean cloth beside the bowl and asked, "Mother, will you be able to wash yourself and change as I head back to town for some food?"

"Yes. I am much better now, Luke. You go ahead, and don't worry about me."

Luke gave her a tender kiss on her forehead and then headed down the hill quickly. Mary took off her dusty outer robe and laid it aside. Next she took off her veil and washed her face and neck with the warm water. She braided her hair with some difficulty, as her hand was very tender, but at last the job was done. Mary rolled her veil into a pillow for her head and exhausted, lay down on her mat, pulled a blanket up to her chin and fell into a deep sleep.

When Luke returned, he busied himself slicing bread and washing dates, all the while humming Mary's favorite tune. She woke up slowly to the lovely sound and smiled and thanked God for sending such a gentle man to keep her safe in her old age. She always trusted in God to meet her needs. She never worried and he never failed her.

Mary lifted herself up on one elbow, and Luke helped her to sit up against the tapestry attached to the stone wall.

"Mother, you are looking much better. I have a nice lunch ready for us."

Then he moved the low table over to Mary. He placed a bowl of dates, a few slices of fresh bread, and several pieces of cheese on the table. Then he brought over two cups of cool water. Luke sat on the floor next to his adopted mother and held her hand as they prayed.

"Dear Father, we thank you for this food, for your love, and for the gifts of the Holy Spirit. We thank you for your Son, Jesus. We love you and look forward to joining you in your kingdom."

They ate slowly, enjoying the sweet taste of the dates and the soft fresh bread. After a while, Luke said, "Mother Mary, tell me a story."

Mary asked, "Which story shall I tell?"

Luke responded as if he were a young boy again. "Start from the beginning. Tell me everything you remember."

Mary laughed. "Haven't you heard these stories enough? I've been telling you stories since I met you many years ago. Don't you get tired of hearing them?"

"Never," Luke replied. "Each time you tell them you remember something new. Each time is like the first time, because you tell the story so well, I feel like I was there. It becomes so real to me. Please tell me a long story. I won't leave you now until John returns, so we have plenty of time. I will find Paul soon enough. I want to remember every detail of your stories. Someday I will write them all down, and others will read them and learn about your son's love and sacrifices. I want everyone to know what I know. I want others to love you and your son as I do. Tell me everything you remember."

Mary put down the piece of fruit she had been nibbling and sighed. "It will take quite a long time to tell everything I remember, but it will help us pass the time. Besides, I love talking about my precious son. I'm so sorry you never knew him."

"But, Mother, I *do* know him! I know him through you and your stories. That's just it. I want others to know him as I do. I love him with all of my heart, and I want others to know and love him as I do. I will continue to paint pictures of you as I imagine you looked as a young woman, the way you looked the day your son died, and the way you look even now. I also want to paint pictures of Jesus to help others know him through your eyes. You have told me how he looked, and I hope I have captured his love in my art."

Mary stroked his face. "Yes, my child. Your paintings have been a great gift to me. They have also been a gift to the disciples as they travel and talk about my son. They leave them with the people they visit to help them understand and learn to love Jesus. I can tell you some of what I remember about Jesus, but you should also get stories from John, Peter, and the others. They were with my precious Jesus many days when I was not. They have stories to tell as well. They have details I do not."

Luke said enthusiastically, "I have been gathering stories since I was a little boy, Mother. Why do you think I always hung around the men like a little mouse? I listened to their stories as I grew up. I learned so much about Jesus! Now I feel him tugging at my heart to write down all that I know."

Mary responded, "Then I will tell you what I remember. But first go back to the well and fill one more jug of water, so we will have enough for the next few days. Buy some fruit, flour, and oil from the market for our next meal. I have some coins here that one of our friends left a few days ago. Go to my chest and look in the bottom corner."

Luke stood up, walked over, and opened the chest. He paused, holding a large bundle of cloth, and walked over to Mary.

"Mother, is this the robe I washed for you fifteen years ago? Is this the robe of our Savior?"

"Yes, my son. It is Jesus' robe, taken from him by the soldiers and saved from the trash pile by you. It still holds the bloodstains from his suffering. It is hard for me to look at, but it gives me comfort to know it is nearby."

Luke put the robe back into the chest reverently. Then he found the coins. "I will be back soon. Take a nap while I am gone, and then we will settle in for a long story."

When Luke left the small hut, Mary stretched out on her mat and reflected on her life. She didn't understand why she was still here on earth. Her son had ascended into heaven fifteen years ago. Before leaving, he had made sure she was in John's protective hands, but still …

he had left. She wondered why she couldn't follow him immediately into heaven. She'd wanted to die the day he had. She knew God had a reason for keeping her alive and on this earth so long. She trusted in his plan, even though she didn't understand it.

It reminded her of the first time she had said yes to God. She had been only a girl—fourteen years old and small for her age. Many people thought she was much younger. The angel's words had been hard to comprehend, but she had given her will totally over to God. Almost fifty years later, she was still doing everything God wanted. She never displeased him. But she still wondered to herself, *Why so long? When can I come home? Why have I been left behind?*

Jesus had told her that she was needed to keep the little band of apostles and disciples together. If Peter was to be the "rock," she needed to be the "glue" that held them together. In the early days, after her son's cruel crucifixion, they all gathered with her in Jerusalem. The apostles and disciples needed to stay close to Mary. They felt guilt and sorrow about leaving her son alone during his agony, and they were determined not to leave his mother. But as much as she needed them, they needed her more. She was so peaceful and trusted in God so much. They were attracted to her love and gentleness, and they had much to learn from her.

After the Holy Spirit had descended on the apostles and disciples, they changed from cowering, weak men to heroes for God. They felt the same peace and strength Mary had demonstrated. They felt the courage to venture beyond the closed doors of the upper room and talk about Jesus. When they were whipped, they rejoiced. When they were imprisoned, their courage and faith grew stronger. Now, fifteen years later, they were beginning to scatter to spread the message of God's love. Now Mary was not needed as she had been in the past. She wondered again why she was still on earth.

She said aloud, as she had said so many times before, "I am your maidservant, Lord. Your Holy Will be done." Then she stretched out on her mat and drifted into a peaceful sleep.

Two hours later, Luke ducked through the low opening to the hut. He went about quietly cleaning up and pouring the water into smaller containers, so the old woman could pour from them.

As she was still sleeping, he went up the trail to his hut higher on the mountain. Three years ago, when he had settled near Ephesus, he'd built a stone hut similar to Mary's and John's, but smaller. When he entered his hut, he gathered some of his things and began preparing food for his journey. He didn't know when John might return, but he wanted to be ready to leave for Caesarea as soon as he could.

As he put together small bundles for the journey, he thought about Paul.

Paul and Luke had developed a special bond. When Paul was converted and joined their small community, he and Luke became close friends. Even though their ages were far apart, they shared much in common. They were both outcasts of a sort; Luke had been a pagan and was not even Jewish. Paul had persecuted some of the first Christians and participated in the murder of Stephen, the first disciple to be killed for his Christian faith. Neither Luke nor Paul had known Jesus before he died. They had never known or been baptized by John the Baptist, and they had both struggled to gain the trust of many of the apostles and other followers of Jesus. Luke felt a special need to help Paul, now that he was in jail.

Luke shook his head and laughed quietly to himself as he thought of Paul and Peter when they had been together years ago. They were so alike and yet so different. They really didn't get along that well. They'd had different opinions about circumcising the Gentile converts and even about circumcising Luke when he was a small boy. Luke remembered that Mary had intervened on his behalf. "Leave the boy alone," she had said as she put a protective arm about his small shoulders. "Can't you see the light of the Holy Spirit in his eyes? He is already a child of God. There is no need for anything more." Luke had, once again, felt protected by this wonderful woman.

He remembered listening to Paul and Peter years ago, discussing rather loudly where they should go to evangelize. They were of different opinions regarding where to travel, but both of them were ready to face any danger, in spite of warnings by the Romans and Jewish leaders. Luke knew they would defend one another to the death, with the same passion with which they disagreed, if the time ever came.

Both Paul and Peter were reckless, impatient, and bold. They were no longer afraid of jail or torture, and in the last several years, they had both endured a lot of it. Luke was afraid they would be killed before long.

There were many others who were passionate about spreading the word of Jesus. John's brother, James, had already been killed for his teaching. Barnabas and Mark had been put in prison and were now released. They were still out there, somewhere, traveling and defying the Romans and high priests. There were many others.

But at this time, Paul needed him, and it was hard for Luke to sit still.

Luke walked the short distance down the hill to Mary's hut and ducked inside. She heard him and turned over. "I think I owe you a long story," she said drowsily.

"Whenever you feel up to it, dear Mother. Take a little more of this water. It is still cool from the well."

He steadied her hand as she sipped the water. He carefully placed the cup on a shelf and said, "Now, let's see how you are healing." He slowly unwrapped the wound on her hand. He gently washed it and fresh blood began to ooze. It was a very deep cut. He took a clean cloth and wrapped it tightly. The blood finally stopped as he pressed his finger on the wound. The bump on her head was going to heal nicely, but her knee was swollen, and a lot of skin had been scraped away. He applied a cool cloth to her knee and bandaged it carefully.

Mary knew that Luke had been helpful to the apostles even as a young boy. Ever since the apostles had begun preaching about Jesus, they had been beaten, whipped, and jailed. When they were released, their first stop was always Mary's little room in Jerusalem. Luke's small gentle hands put salve on their whipped backs and cold water on their bruises. He set broken bones and sewed deep cuts. All of the lessons he had learned about healing in Antioch and Pilate's palace were put to good use among the small group of followers.

As he finished tending to Mary's wounds, he kissed her on the forehead and said, "Now I am ready for a rest and a long story."

Mary arranged herself on her mat and began.

CHAPTER THREE

BECOMING A WOMAN

When I was a young girl of fourteen, my parents, Anne and Joachim, had arranged a marriage for me to a man named Joseph. He was a kind man, but the idea of marriage frightened me. Joseph was much older—about twice my age—and I knew nothing about men. I knew how to cook and keep a house, but I still enjoyed children's games and long talks with my friends. I was still a girl, and I was afraid of the idea of becoming someone's wife and eventually someone's mother.

I shared a small room with my cousin, Mary Salome. There was just enough space for our two mats with a window in between. There were two pegs on the wall on which to hang our clothes and bags. There was a small shelf where we kept little odds-and-ends and a jar of fresh water in one corner. Salome slept against one wall, and I slept against the other. Both of her parents had died the year before from a sickness that spread throughout Nazareth. Her mother had been Anne's sister.

Mary paused in her story and closed her eyes as she remembered that night forty-nine years before. "Do you remember Salome, Luke? She was a few years older than I and was my best friend. I loved her very much."

"Yes, Mother, I remember her. She was the mother of James, Joseph, Simon, and Jude. She was very kind to me when I first came to live with you."

Mary continued, "Her husband took me into their home some of the times when I couldn't follow Jesus as he traveled throughout Galilee. She was with me in Jerusalem during those last days of my son's life. She stayed with me all through that horrible night when Jesus was arrested and all through the next day when my son was tortured and killed. She helped me wash his body that Friday afternoon. Salome stayed close to me after my son's death, and she and John took very good care of me throughout those sad days.

"Did I ever tell you how many bowls of water we used to wash his body? I still see that in my dreams: bowls and bowls of dark, red water. They kept filling up with blood so quickly! There was a young man with us, but I never knew his name. He was there at the foot of the cross the last hour of my son's death. He helped Joseph, John, and Nicodemus take Jesus' body down. He climbed the ladder to take the nails from his hands. Then he and John gently lowered my son's precious body to the men below who had already taken out the nails from his feet. The young man helped me take the thorns from my son's head as I held him in my lap for the last time. He cried with me as we carried him to the flat stone just outside the tomb to wash his body. That same man ran to the well over and over to fill the jug with water. It took so much water to wash away his blood."

Mary looked up, her eyes glistening with tears. "I'm sorry. I seem to have gotten away from my story."

One night I lay on my cot thinking about Joseph and praying to God that I might know His will for my life. I told God about my fears, but I promised that I would do my best if that was what He wanted of me. After my prayer, I whispered, 'Salome, are you awake?' I wanted to talk to her about Joseph and my promise to God. She stirred and rolled over, but she did not answer me.

Just as I was about to fall asleep, I heard a rush of wind or something moving just outside our window. I looked across the room where my cousin lay. Salome was breathing softly and sleeping soundly. I looked out the window and the trees and bushes were not stirring. It was a still night. I sat up and strained to see in the dark.

Then I saw a bright light just inside our window. A very tall, strong-looking man appeared within the light. The light surrounded him and was as bright as the sun, but it did not hurt my eyes to look at him. He had golden hair that fell in soft curls to his shoulders. His eyes were light blue, and he had wings. The wings were not made of feathers like a bird. They were made of thin skin like the transparent wings of a dragonfly. As the light hit them, they reflected different colors. He had a kind face, and he smiled at me. In spite of his beautiful smile, I was very frightened. I thought it was my time to die, and God had sent an angel to take me from this earth. I curled into the tightest ball I could against the wall, covered up with my blanket, and closed my eyes tightly. I wondered what Salome was seeing, but I was afraid to call out to her or open my eyes.

When the angel began to speak, his voice was like beautiful music. He told me not to be frightened. He said his name was Gabriel. My muscles relaxed; I pushed the blanket off my face and looked at him again. I glanced over to where Salome was, but she was still asleep. I wondered how she could sleep through the bright light and the sound of his voice.

He smiled at me and said that the Almighty had selected me to be the mother of the Savior of the world. I was stunned. I was no longer frightened, but I was overwhelmed and puzzled. I asked the angel, "How can this be? I am a virgin. I have not known a man." I was also thinking, "Why me? I could never be the mother of the Savior. I am far too young and simple."

The Angel said that if I chose to follow the will of the Father, the power of the Holy Spirit would come over me, and I would conceive a son, and that his name would be Jesus. I still didn't understand what all of this meant, but I did know that if I said yes, my life would change in ways I could not even begin to comprehend. I also understood that I could say no, and my life would go on in a normal way without complications and difficulties.

I understood that God would love me no matter which decision I made. This was my choice. I had free will. But hadn't I just finished a prayer asking to know God's will? Now a very beautiful angel was telling me what God's will was. The message was clear.

My mother and father had taught me all my life that if I put my faith in God, all would be well. I did not feel worthy of such an honor or capable of such a duty. I could not imagine why God had chosen me, but I told the angel, "I am the handmaiden of the Lord. I am willing to accept whatever He wants. His will be done unto me." I felt very peaceful after saying those words. It was the same feeling I remembered as a very young child when I fell asleep in my mother's arms. I felt loved and protected.

Then Gabriel told me that I must travel to the house of my cousin Elizabeth. He said that she was six months with child, even though she was old and had been barren. I remembered the story about Abraham and Sarah and did not doubt that this could be possible if God ordained it.

Gabriel smiled once more and then dissolved in the light.

I looked over at Mary Salome. She was still sleeping. I lay down on my mat and began to pray deeply from my heart. I felt a sense of inner peace that I had never felt before, as the Holy Spirit filled me completely with his love. I felt such joy! I could never explain the feeling with words. I entered into deep prayer with the Lord that lasted until dawn. When light finally came into the room, I began to dress quietly. I was not frightened anymore, as I knew God would help me. I had changed from a girl to a woman in a few hours. I was no longer afraid to be Joseph's wife or someone's mother; even if that someone happened to be the long awaited Savior.

I found my mother, Anne, in our main room. She was preparing for our breakfast. I went to her, kissed her cheek, held her hand, and told her about the visit from Gabriel. Something in my eyes and the tone of my voice convinced her that this had not been a dream; it had been real. She saw the change in me. I was no longer a playful child; I was a woman who had accepted a great responsibility. She suggested that I tell Joseph right away.

I walked across our small village and found Joseph working in his wood shop. He was bent over, making a chest for our new home.

Mary looked up from her story and pointed to the old chest in her hut. "That's the one over in the corner. Remember the trouble it was, getting it from Jerusalem to my hut here on this mountain?" Luke nodded as he remembered his struggles finding porters to carry the chest over the mountain. "Yes, Mother, it was difficult, but I knew it was very important to you and to all of us. I love it. I like to imagine Joseph as he made it for you. I can picture Jesus as a little boy, sitting on it and climbing into it for fun. I am very happy we were able to keep it all of these years."

Luke stood up and walked over to the chest. "Mother, what would you have us do with this chest and the objects inside after you are gone?"

As soon as he spoke, he was embarrassed by his question, but Mary answered without any evidence of concern. "Whatever John decides is best."

Luke returned to his seat on the floor and Mary continued her story.

I stood in the doorway of Joseph's hut and remained silent, watching him work. He was a nice-looking man. He was a little taller than my father. He had curly, dark-brown hair, beautiful dark-brown eyes, and a straight and narrow nose. He had strong muscles in his arms and legs from his years of hard work. His skin was darker than mine, and fine grains of wood dust were clinging to the small hairs on his arms and legs. He was concentrating on his job, sanding one side of the wood to a smooth finish.

When he looked up, he smiled at me and put down his tool. He came over to me and took my hand gently. "Why, Mary, what a wonderful surprise to see you this morning. You look beautiful with the sun at your back. It is as if you are glowing with your own light. Have you had your breakfast yet? I was just about to eat some bread and cheese."

I told him I would love to sit with him as he ate. I nibbled on the bread but was too excited to eat. I finally told him the story of the angel's visit and that I had conceived a child through the power of the Holy Spirit. I told him that this child would be the Savior. He stopped eating and looked at me strangely. I had never seen that expression on his face before. I could not tell what he was thinking.

He rose slowly and turned from me. "I need to pray about what to do," was all he said in a very somber tone. I went closer to him and he moved away. "Go home now, Mary," he said firmly. His tone was cold, and his body had become rigid. My heart was broken. He did not believe me. He did not embrace me and rejoice in this child as I had hoped he would. I ran home to my mother as tears began to fill my eyes.

"Joseph doesn't believe me, Mother. I don't know what to do!" I wailed as I burst into the room. "Well, Daughter, if you are following God's will, He will help Joseph understand. Don't worry about the road ahead. You have chosen the right path. If Joseph is not meant to take the journey with you, then that is that."

My father, Joachim, had been sitting at the table, staring at his uneaten breakfast. My mother had told him what had happened to me during the night. He was stunned by the news, but did not think I was lying. I had never lied in my life; and to lie about the Savior would be an unpardonable sin. He was just very confused and worried about me.

I touched his shoulder, said nothing, and went to my room. I found Salome sitting on her mat. She had overheard everything. I lay on my mat, exhausted, and continued to cry. She held me tight and stroked my hair. She believed every word I had said. She had never known me to lie or even to joke about such things. My mother and father then came into our room and suggested we all pray together. My father led the prayer. He asked God to guide our lives and to help Joseph understand.

Joseph came to our home a couple of hours later. My family gathered together as he stood in the doorway. He was very stiff and looked tired. He said that I had disappointed him and misled him. He said he had believed I was a sweet, timid, and holy girl; and now his dreams for our life together had been shattered.

He said I must have made up the childish lie about an angel's visit to cover up my shame. He told me he would have the betrothal dissolved quietly. I ran to him and grabbed his hand. It was cold, and he held his fingers together in a tight fist. I begged him not to divorce me. I told him it was God's will that he help me to raise my son. Joseph looked at me sadly and said nothing. He gently pulled his hand from mine as a tear slowly rolled down his cheek. Then he turned and walked out of our hut.

Joseph went to one of the elders of our small temple in Nazareth and asked him for assistance in dissolving the anticipated union. He was told to never see me again and to find another wife as soon as possible. The elder was not a man who could keep confidences, and our town was a small one. By the next day, most people in our village had heard that Joseph, a righteous man, was seeking a divorce. Many people guessed that I was with child and talked about sending me away or even stoning me. I tell you the truth: Satan would have loved to see me and my unborn child dead! He was working through the hearts of many people in Nazareth those days.

The next evening, Joseph was in his home praying, as the elder's advice had not brought him peace. He fell into a deep sleep as he prayed, and

Gabriel visited Joseph in a dream. Praise God! The angel said, "Joseph, son of David, do not be afraid to take Mary as your wife. It is through the Holy Spirit that this child has been conceived within her. She will bear a son and you are to name him Jesus, because he will save his people from their sins."

Before the sun came up that morning, Joseph rushed to our home and shared his dream with my family. He held me tight and said how sorry he was for having doubted me. We all wept for joy, and then we arranged for a quiet wedding immediately.

We did not have the usual wedding feast that most people had. Our family was plagued by this scandal. The people of Nazareth were talking about my disgrace and would not have attended if we had invited them. We just celebrated with my mother, father, and my cousin Mary Salome. Joseph's family did not even attend. His parents and his brother and his brother's wife all believed that Joseph was making a grave mistake by marrying me. They did not speak to us until years later when we returned from our exile in Egypt.

The same elder who had spread the rumors about me officiated at our wedding. All through the ceremony, he shook his head and would not look at me. He thought I was not worthy of Joseph and tried again to talk him out of the marriage. It was a very sad day for my mother and father, as they had hoped for a joyous celebration. Now they, as well as my cousin, had already received harsh criticism from the villagers. Many women stopped talking to my mother and Salome. My father lost not only friends but much of the income he derived from selling his goat milk and cheese. My family suffered because of my decision, but they did it with glad hearts, as they knew we were doing what God wanted.

Joseph did not take me to his bed after our wedding. We both knew that our marriage would be different; that we were called to a higher purpose. Our job was to bring the Christ child safely into the world and to raise him in a loving home. Joseph loved me as a dear brother loves his sister, not as a husband loves a wife.

"Do you understand what I am saying, Luke?" Mary looked deep into Luke's eyes.

"Yes, Mother." Luke was a bit embarrassed by this question. He remained silent for a while and then said, "Mother, is that why many of the people in Nazareth, and even here in Ephesus, have been so cruel to you, even after all these years? Do they think that you are a sinful woman?" It was hard for Luke to imagine, as he had always known Mary to be a pure, kind, and gentle woman.

"Yes, I'm afraid so. People in the grasp of Satan do not forget a scandal easily. They gossip to make themselves feel more important. They do not understand the love of my son. I pray for them each day to open their hearts to God's love. If they could only know how much my son loves them and has sacrificed for them, they could yet be saved. If they would only ask for his forgiveness, he would embrace them and spend eternity with them. That is what he desires for all of his brothers and sisters.

"It all began so many years ago. It seemed like all of Nazareth turned their backs on my little family. When I left our hut, children would follow me, calling me names and sometimes throwing stones. My mother became concerned for my safety and the safety of my unborn child. She encouraged Joseph to take me to visit our cousin Elizabeth soon after our wedding, as Gabriel had told me to do."

Luke held her hands and said, "Dear Mother, you look tired. Let me get you another drink of water, and then I want you to rest. I will leave for a little while and try to find out where John is. I will be back in a few hours."

Mary squeezed Luke's hand and said, "Let us pray. Dear Father, we ask you to touch the hearts of those who do not know your love. Please forgive those who have hurt my family with their insults and blows. Please protect and strengthen Luke, Paul, John, Peter, and all the other followers of my son. Give them the courage and fortitude to follow Your Holy Will, even though they will receive insults and suffer for doing so."

Luke gave her a gentle kiss next to the cut on her forehead and helped her to her mat. He arranged a cover for her and put a cup of water close by. He grabbed a quick drink of water for himself from the full jug and quickly walked out through the door.

He walked to the home of Aquila and Priscilla, two of the first Christians in Ephesus, but they were not home.

He needed someone to stay with Mary until John returned. Luke felt an urgent need to leave for Caesarea to help Paul. He could find no one nearby that he could trust. When he returned to Mary's hut, it was almost dark. She was sound asleep and in the same position she had been when he'd left hours before. He rolled out John's mat and placed it before the entrance to the tiny hut. He eased himself down slowly. He did not realize how tired he was until he finally let himself rest. The last thought he had before drifting off to sleep was how frightened he had been when he first found his dear Mother lying unconscious in the dust on the side of the road. Luke said a short prayer that Mary would always be cared for while she was still on this earth, and he quickly fell into a deep sleep.

CHAPTER FOUR

TWO BABY BOYS

Mary awoke after a deep sleep to the heat of mid-morning. She was thirsty again, but there was plenty of fresh water—Luke had made sure of that. He had even left a cup of water beside her mat. She could smell bread baking in the oven outside, and her stomach rumbled with hunger. "Luke must have been up early this morning making bread and fetching water," she thought. She leaned up on her elbow and took a slow sip, then put down the small cup. "He is such a thoughtful young man!" she said aloud.

"And who are you talking about, Mother?" The deep baritone voice came from the doorway. The sun was behind him, and Mary couldn't see his face, but she knew it was Barnabas by his voice and hulking shape.

Mary rose slowly from her mat. Her joints were stiff, and her knee was still swollen and sore from the fall yesterday morning. She finally stood up and hobbled toward him. She embraced him and exclaimed, "Barnabas, it is so good to see you! How are you? Do you know about Paul? Luke told me he has been arrested."

Barnabas did not release the embrace quickly. This woman was dearer to him than anyone else on earth, and he warmed in her presence. Finally, with reluctance, he let her go and brushed a hand through his shaggy hair. "Yes, that is true about Paul. He is in prison in Caesarea. I came to lead Luke to him. And how are you doing, Mother?"

"Oh, I'm fine … and better now that you are here," she said warmly.

Mary stepped back to examine Barnabas. She could tell with one look that he had been walking for several days with very little rest. He had dark circles under his deep-set black eyes. Dirt and twigs were still tangled in his course black hair from sleeping on the ground, and he moved slowly. Mary guessed that he had not eaten a warm meal in several days. She imagined he had been gathering whatever he could find growing wild, or eating what others would share with him. Barnabas was a large man and always hungry, even when food was plenty.

"Well, first you must wash away the dust from your journey. Then you will rest here and eat. You have traveled a long way."

Barnabas nodded and walked outside to wash his face and hands in the bowl of water Mary poured for him. He placed the bowl on the large flat rock, and Mary followed him with a clean towel.

Barnabas leaned over and splashed his face with the cold water. Then he rubbed his hands together to wipe away the dust from the journey. Mary handed him the towel as he looked around and asked, "Are you alone, Mother? Where is Luke? Where is John?"

"John left five days ago to try to help Peter, who is also in prison."

Barnabas continued to rub his face and beard vigorously with the towel. When finished, he handed Mary the very soiled towel and said, "Again? That man is like a lion. He fears nothing! He will be in God's kingdom before any of us if he keeps aggravating those in power."

Mary just shook her head and said quietly, "Peter was not always brave, but he has grown in love and faith over the years. The Holy Spirit gives him courage now. He was born with a stubborn streak, as you well know. He is one of the most tenacious, hard-headed, and impatient men I have ever known … although Paul comes close. With prayer, however, Peter grows every day in God's love and, as hard as it is to believe, in patience as well." With that, Mary laughed heartily.

Barnabas chuckled and put his hands on Mary's cheeks and rested his forehead against her forehead in a gesture of affection and respect. "Oh, Mother, it is good to see you again. I miss your laughter and your love so much when I am away. I wish I could stay here all the time to take care of you and just be near you. Now may we go inside and eat? I can finish washing later. I'm as hungry as a bear!"

Mary nodded and went into the hut. She took a flat block of smooth wood and a sharp knife from one of the shelves and put them on the low table. Mary bent over the small box beside the door and took out a thick piece of cloth. Then she went back to the fire pit and moved the embers away from the oven. She opened the iron door using the cloth and, shifting it into both hands, took out the bread. She brought the bread back into the house and put it on the wooden slab. She waved the rag to cool it a bit as Barnabas watched hungrily. Finally, she began slicing it into thick pieces.

"Now, my son, sit and eat."

Barnabas sat down gratefully, and Mary handed him a large piece of bread with a goblet of cool water. After his first satisfying bite, he said, "Where is Luke? I passed his hut on the way down the hill and didn't see him. Don't tell me *he* has also been arrested."

Mary sat on her mat and leaned against the wall padded with an old coverlet that John had hung for her. "No, Luke is still here in Ephesus. He is probably in the village seeking information about Paul. He thought Timothy or Erasmus might know. He was also going to visit the silversmith, Demetrius. He isn't a Christian, but he knows much news of the world outside our village. Out-of-town visitors usually stop in his shop. Demetrius is the best source of information regarding arrests or pardons or marriages … or just about anything."

Mary paused to take a sip of water. "I'm glad you are here, Barnabas. Luke could use a friend now. Will you travel with him to Caesarea?"

"Yes, Mother, I promise to take care of your little Luke. But first I need to go outside and take off some of these robes. It's getting rather warm, and I'm bringing half of the dirt from my journey into your tidy hut." With that, he swallowed the last bite of his slice of bread and walked outside. He removed his outer cloak, gave it a good shake over the hillside, and then laid it aside on a large, flat rock.

Mary searched in her chest for the ivory comb she had been given as a gift from one of the visiting kings many years ago. When she found it, she poured out another cup of water for Barnabas and followed him outside.

He accepted the water gratefully and finished it off in two swallows. Mary watched in amazement. This man was so large but like a child in many ways. She scooped up the heavy cloak and examined it. It was caked with mud and had several tears. She put the cloak back on the rock, handed Barnabas the comb, and went back into her hut for a small brush.

Barnabas sat on the rock and began the slow process of combing out his hair and beard. It had not been properly combed for quite some time and was full of tangles and bits of earthy things.

Mary walked back outside and joined him on the rock. She carefully brushed off the mud from his cloak, trying not to lengthen any of the existing tears. Mary enjoyed looking after those who followed her son. She was truly a mother to so many.

"After you have combed your hair and beard, go into the chest and take out John's spare robe. I will mend and wash these garments for you before you leave again." Barnabas nodded and then gritted his teeth as he pulled at a particularly snarled bit of hair.

They sat in companionable silence as they gazed down the hill and continued their tasks. It was a beautiful view. They could see parts of the town below and mountain ridges in the distance. It was cooler up here, quiet and peaceful. There were lovely splashes of white, pink, and purple wildflowers with white trees dotting the hill side.

When they heard footsteps on the trail leading from town, Barnabas stood up quickly and spotted Luke climbing toward them. His arms were full of jugs, packages, and baskets. Barnabas' stomach growled once again as he imagined the food they contained.

Luke's eyes were cast downward, watching his steps on the steep terrain. Suddenly he looked up and saw Barnabas standing there like a giant with his hands on his hips. Luke quickened his pace and ran the last few steps. When he arrived at the rock, he put down his packages and gave Barnabas a hearty hug. Luke talked quickly. "I'm so glad to see you! No one seems to know where Paul has been taken. I'm very worried."

Barnabas stumbled back and laughed. "I think I'm going to call you Little Paul! You get so excited! Don't worry. I just came from the prison where they are keeping him. He is well enough, and I'm sure he will live for a while longer. Paul asked me to bring you back as soon as possible, however. I left him with plenty of papyrus sheets, lamb skins, and ink, and he is writing letters now. He wants you to deliver them to our friends in the cities in which he has established churches. You are one of the best people for the job because so many people know and respect you." He paused and winked at Mary. "But I see you have a very important job now."

"Yes, and I'm afraid I can't leave her until John returns or we find someone reliable to stay with her." Luke said this without thinking and immediately wished he had not spoken within earshot of Mary.

Mary listened to the conversation with a sad heart. She realized she had become a burden to those who loved her. She was interfering with the work her son had left for these men to do.

"Now, Mother," Barnabas said gruffly while turning to Mary and giving her shoulders a little squeeze, "do not let this distress you. I am too tired to leave any time soon. I need at least a day or two to recover my strength."

He gave Luke an admonishing look over Mary's shoulder. They both knew that Barnabas was a strong man and did not need much of a recuperative rest, but his look told Luke not to protest. He continued, "Let Luke prepare our midday meal, and we will have a nice chat. That little piece of bread did not fill up even one part of my stomach! I am still famished!"

That remark caused Mary to smile and warmed both their hearts.

Embarrassed by his remark, Luke picked up his packages and went into the hut to prepare a hearty meal.

Mary stood up, put the cloak and brush down on the smooth, flat rock where she had been sitting, and went over to the large jug of water.

She filled the wash bowl with fresh water and motioned Barnabas to sit back down on the rock. She brought the bowl over carefully and set it down at the base of the rock. She squatted beside the bowl and began to remove his sandals. Barnabas knew it was useless to protest. Mary often did this for visitors as an act of humility. To deny her this was to deny her an opportunity to follow her son's example.

He watched her pale, slender fingers move gracefully, untying his sandals and laying them aside. Then she put each foot in the bowl, one at a time. Mary noticed a bad cut on his left foot and she was particularly gentle washing it clean. Barnabas flinched but didn't protest. Mary rubbed hard where the dirt was caked after many days of hard walking. Then she dried his feet thoroughly and was tying on the last sandal when Luke stepped out of the hut.

"Our meal is ready whenever you are finished."

Barnabas, blushing, stood up quickly and helped Mary to her feet. He took the bowl, emptied it into the nearest patch of flowers, and placed it back beside the door. Then he followed Mary into the cool hut and helped her down onto her mat beside the table.

When they had all been seated and said a prayer of thanksgiving, Luke began to pass the fruit he had bought that morning and what was left of the bread. There was a jug of clean water on the floor beside the table and a goblet for each.

Luke poured out the water, and Barnabas drained his cup quickly; he was still very thirsty from his travels on dusty roads.

Barnabas took a huge bite of his tough bread, chewed on it slowly, enjoying the flavor, and finally swallowed. Then he took a large drink of water and asked, "Which story will we hear today, dear Mother?"

Mary laughed at the question. The men laughed with her. Her voice was always gentle and wonderful to hear, but her laughter was something even more special. It was like singing birds on a beautiful spring morning—only better. It made everyone who heard it smile, even when times were sad.

Luke answered excitedly, "Mary was telling me the story of when Jesus was born."

"Oh, I love that story!" Barnabas exploded. He gave Mary a squeeze around her shoulders and nearly knocked her over. Sometimes he forgot just how big he was and how small and frail Mary had become. "Precious Mother, I am so sorry," Barnabas said as he helped her regain her balance. Mary smiled like a shy child. "No harm done," she said as she patted his arm. She straightened her veil, picked up the piece of bread that had fallen, and held it like a treasure.

She remembered how many times in her life a piece of bread *was* a treasure. She remembered how she and Joseph would split a small loaf as they traveled. Other times she would give away most of her share to others who were hungry. Giving was a way of life for her; she always thought of herself last.

She broke the piece of bread she held now in half and passed the larger part to Barnabas, as he had already eaten his share. Barnabas took it and nodded gratefully.

"Now, let me see," she said as she nodded in return. "I was just about to tell the story of our visit with Elizabeth."

It was not an easy trip from Nazareth to Zachariah's home in the hill country of Judah. The road was dusty and dangerous. It was April, so the weather was mild. We did not meet with any misfortune along the way. There were no thieves or accidents, so we made the trip in only three days. I could walk quickly and did not require much rest, as I was not yet experiencing the signs of motherhood. Joseph was still young and very strong.

Mary's eyes began to glaze as memories flooded back to her. She missed Joseph so much. Perhaps, if he were still alive, she would not be such a burden to these men. She fell silent, lost in her own thoughts, and the men sat quietly as they ate and waited. They watched her eyes glisten with tears while she remembered her dead husband. Then she swallowed a bite of bread, took a sip of water, and continued.

When we arrived in the village of Jutta, we went directly to Ein Kerem, Zachariah's family home. One of Zachariah's house servants said that he and Elizabeth had moved to their summer home early, as Elizabeth was already suffering from the heat. You see, Zachariah was a high priest and was well-to-do. He and Elizabeth had two homes: one at the foot of the hill in the village and a summer home at the top of the hill. It was much cooler up there, with wonderful breezes.

When I traveled there as a child, I always preferred the home on top of the hill, even though it was made from a simple cave. It was so beautiful up there. You could look down on several valleys below and see other hills far away. Elizabeth was a wonderful cook as well. She never had children of her own, so when my mother would take me to visit, she would give me special treats. I especially loved her bread. I don't know her secret, but it was the best bread I ever tasted.

As Joseph and I climbed the steep hill to her home, I could smell bread baking. I think somehow she knew I was coming, and she was baking it just for me—just as she had done when I was a small child. As we stood in the doorway, I saw Elizabeth sitting on the ground, kneading another loaf of dough on a flat rock.

I called to her as we entered their home. When she heard my voice, she put her hand on her swollen belly and stood up slowly. Before I could reach her, she cried out in a loud voice, "Most blessed are you among women, and blessed is the fruit of your womb." When Elizabeth embraced me, she said, "And how does this happen to me, that the mother of my Lord should come to me? For at the moment the sound of your greeting reached my ears, the infant in my womb leaped for joy. Blessed are you who believed that what was spoken to you by the Lord would be fulfilled."

The others in the room, even Joseph, were amazed at these words. Gabriel had only visited me two weeks before, so no one could tell by looking at me that I carried a child.

Zachariah completely understood what Elizabeth meant when she said, "Blessed are you who believed," for he had been punished for his own disbelief. Six months earlier, when Zachariah was in the temple, an angel of the Lord had appeared and told him that Elizabeth would bear a son in her old age. Zachariah was told to name his son John. At that time, Zachariah doubted the Lord could do such a wondrous thing, as his wife was barren and beyond the age of childbearing. He had been struck dumb for his unbelief.

As he saw me and heard Elizabeth's words, tears began running down his face. The Holy Spirit filled him with the knowledge that he had been *privileged to witness not one but two miracles. Two boy babies would be born to this family: one the Savior, born to a virgin, and one to prepare others for the Savior, born to a barren, old woman.*

Zachariah had seen the face of God's angel and had felt God's disappointment in him. He was determined never to disappoint God again. He would do whatever he could to protect both the women before him and the babies they held inside their wombs.

He and Joseph stood shoulder to shoulder with an understanding of their important roles in the lives of the two children who would be born.

Barnabas and Luke watched Mary's face brighten as she remembered the reunion with Elizabeth. Her voice rose in pitch as she repeated the words she had said forty-nine years earlier.

I felt the presence of the Holy Spirit so deeply, and my joy spilled out with words: "My soul proclaims the greatness of the Lord; my spirit rejoices in God my Savior, for He has looked upon His handmaid's lowliness. Behold, from now on, all ages will call me blessed. The Mighty One has done great things for me. Holy is His name!"

I could hold back tears of joy no longer, and I embraced Elizabeth for a long time. She was the only one who truly understood what I was feeling. We knew that our children were special gifts from God, and I had finally found someone who could completely share my joy. You see, my mother, father, cousin and Joseph were still worried about my pregnancy. They did not completely understand what was happening to me; Elizabeth did.

Our visit to Ein Kerem helped Joseph understand all that God had in store for us.

Joseph stayed in Zachariah's home for four days, after which he left with a party of travelers to return to Nazareth. He had much work to do to prepare for our home. He also wanted to bring news back to my parents of my safe arrival to Jutta. Joseph knew he was leaving me in good care. As we said goodbye, he promised to return in three months to take me back to Nazareth.

For the next twelve weeks, Elizabeth and I comforted each other. Sometimes we would lie together on our mats during the heat of the day and talk about the special children we were carrying. We talked about what they might be like as men. We made plans to visit one another as much as possible as our sons grew to manhood.

Sometimes, as we walked together into the small village near Elizabeth's house, she was ridiculed for being pregnant at her age. She responded to this behavior with humility and silence. I admired her for her courage. She taught me a great deal about how to behave when neighbors are cruel.

All through the last three months of her pregnancy, Elizabeth and her maid taught me important lessons. Elizabeth's maid, Sarah, was the mother of five children and a grandmother of fifteen. She had assisted at the birth of all of her grandchildren, so she knew quite a lot about things Elizabeth and I had never experienced. Sarah taught me what I should eat to ensure a healthy baby. She taught me how to sleep, sit, and stand with a swollen belly. As Elizabeth's time came to deliver her child, Sarah taught me about labor pains and giving birth.

I was with Elizabeth from the beginning of her labor to the end. It was the first time I had seen a baby born! Sarah showed me how to clean out the baby's nose and mouth and help him breathe. She showed me how to tie the cord and cut it with a sharp knife that had been cleaned in the fire. Then Sarah handed the newborn baby to me as she took care of Elizabeth after the birth. I washed the blood from his tiny body and gave him to Elizabeth to suckle. Sarah taught Elizabeth and me how to care for a newborn infant. I listened carefully, even though I thought my mother and cousin would be with me when my time came. As it happened, I don't know what I would have done, alone in Bethlehem, without those lessons.

After John was born, Zachariah spoke for the first time in nine months. He told us all about the visit from Gabriel. I got very excited as he described the vision, for I realized that it was the same angel who had visited me. We talked and prayed together all through that blessed night.

As we watched a healthy baby sleep, we thanked the good God for all He had done for us. A barren, old woman had given birth to a child who was destined to help my son. I had been blessed to carry the Christ child within my womb. I had learned valuable lessons about the cruelty of others and how to live with verbal abuse from neighbors. I had learned how to care for myself and a newborn baby. Joseph and Zachariah had grown in faith and trust in God and his messengers.

We talked about how God knows what is best for us. Sometimes His Holy Will seems difficult to follow, but it is always the best path, even if it is strewn with rocks and deep holes. We just need to pray, listen to his quiet voice within, and follow where he leads.

Mary paused in her story, bowed her head, and began praying silently. Barnabas and Luke did the same. The men prayed for an increase in faith, as they knew they would face many trials. They prayed in thanksgiving for the faith they already had and for this precious Mother in their midst. When they looked up, they saw Mary smiling and looking at them the way a proud Mother looks on her children who please her.

"You are wise to pray often," she said to them. The more you pray, the closer you become to the Almighty, and the more strength you will have for your long journeys. Never put aside prayer for other things. Never forget the power of prayer. God is always listening to you and has his arms outstretched to embrace you."

Barnabas reached for a fig and said to Mary, "Would you like to rest now, Mother? You look tired."

"Yes, I think I am ready for a nap." Mary finished the fig she had been eating and moved from the table onto her mat. Barnabas covered her with a blanket, and he and Luke walked out into the sunshine as Mary rested her eyes.

They discussed travel plans and what they should do when they arrived in Caesarea. They knew they would need money to pay for their passage across the sea. They might also need money to pay for Paul's release. They discussed how they might earn or borrow enough money for what was necessary.

When they came back into the hut, they found Mary making a drink of water and balsam. "That looks wonderful, Mother. Did you make enough for all of us?"

"Of course, I did," Mary said, pouring out three goblets of the drink. Then she walked over to her chest, leaned over, and pulled out a carefully wrapped object of some weight. As she pulled the cloth from the object, the men found themselves staring in wonder at a block of gold.

Mary said quietly, "Take this to Demetrius in town. He will give you a fair price for it. It should be enough for you to travel to Caesarea and pay for Paul's release."

The men began to protest, but one look at Mary silenced them. "I need this no longer. I have been saving it for forty-eight years, and I sense that this is the purpose for which it was given. Now, would you like me to continue my story?"

"Please, yes," the men said in unison. Luke wrapped the gold bar in the cloth and put it in a corner under his blanket. Then they all arranged themselves on the floor, and Mary resumed her story.

When Joseph and I returned to Nazareth after the visit with Elizabeth, things were not easy. In Zachariah's house, those who loved me and understood my pregnancy had protected me. The rest of the townspeople did not know that I was with child. Back in my hometown of Nazareth, people were still gossiping. It hurt to hear such talk, but I had learned from Elizabeth to respond in silence and humility. Joseph had built our home very close to my mother's, and I was able to stay inside most of the time. Others in the family went to the well, gathered firewood, and did all of the outside chores. No one wanted to expose me or my unborn baby to danger.

Six months later, we learned that a decree had gone out from Caesar Augustus that a census was to be taken. Joseph and I were ordered to travel to Judea to the city of Bethlehem. It was not a good time for me to be traveling and riding on a donkey. Joseph requested an exemption, but he was a poor carpenter with very little influence, and so we were resigned to go.

My mother was very worried, but I had faith that we were doing what God had planned. Joseph sold what he could and then closed up his little shop. He took items of value that he had not been able to sell or didn't want to sell, like my chest, to my parents' home. Then he tried to borrow money for a cart so I could ride in more comfort. He was not able to collect enough money for that, so we took my father's donkey. The donkey carried me and our supplies for the trip. Joseph walked. My mother wept for me as we left her home; she was so worried.

This trip was much harder than the first one we had made several months earlier. By now, I was large with my baby. I had to stop more frequently to rest, and our journey took over five days instead of the usual three. *Each time we rested by the side of the road, we would watch the people pass by on their way to Bethlehem. Those who knew Joseph or his family would stop and talk to us and offer food and water. The women looked at me with compassion. I just could not find a comfortable way to ride or sleep. Sometimes it was easier to walk than to ride that donkey, but then I would tire and have to rest. Joseph did his best to help me, but there was really not much he could do. He was very worried about me and the baby. He also knew that with each family group that passed us as we rested, we lost an opportunity for shelter once we reached Bethlehem. He knew it was a small town, and there would be few rooms to rent.*

I was not sleeping well on the ground, and two of the nights we tried to sleep, it rained. We were soaked through, and I shivered uncontrollably those long cold nights.

When we were only a few hours from Bethlehem, I began to feel the first pangs of labor. My mother and Elizabeth had tried to prepare me for this experience, but now that it was happening, I became frightened. I was far from shelter and the comfort of my mother's arms. I think Joseph was even more frightened than I was. He tried not to let me see his concern, but I knew him well enough by then to read his expressions. When that crease between his eyes deepened, he was worried. When he stopped trying to make me laugh, he was worried. He hadn't joked since the downpour the night before, and the crease between his eyes was very deep.

I tried to hide my pains from him at first, but as they intensified, it became obvious that I could no longer ride the donkey. Joseph was able to talk a passing traveler into letting me climb into his wagon and stretch out on bags of grain for the last two hours of the journey.

By the time we reached Bethlehem, it was after dark. Joseph and the man helped me out of the cart, and I sat on the side of the street, holding the donkey's reins while Joseph walked off to find us a room. Because we were among the last to arrive in the small village, Joseph could not find a place to stay. He tried several public houses, but they were all full. It was long after dark, and my labor was becoming more frequent. Joseph became desperate.

He came back for me and helped me walk to the last possible shelter on the outskirts of the village. I rested against the door post as Joseph rapped loudly on the door. We could tell that we had roused the innkeeper from his sleep when he answered the door with a scowl. He barely looked at us and announced that there was no room. He started to slam the door closed, but Joseph put his foot in the doorway. He insisted that we be given entry. Joseph said we would sleep in the kitchen if we must, but we needed to get out of the cold night air. The innkeeper became very aggravated with Joseph's persistence and pushed him out into the street and slammed the door.

My poor husband fell backwards, scraping his elbow on the rocky ground. Joseph just lay there bleeding. He had been walking since before the sun came up that morning and hadn't stopped for food. He had given me most of the water. He began weeping from exhaustion, worry, and frustration. He felt like a total failure as a husband and father.

I went over to Joseph and began wiping his arm with the end of my veil. He looked tenderly up to me and sobbed, "I'm so sorry; I'm so sorry." He couldn't say anything else. He had reached the end of his strength and had no more ideas. He knew my child was coming soon, as I moaned and clutched my stomach. I could feel the baby trying to come out.

At that moment the door of the inn opened, and a large woman with a kind face stepped out. She watched us for a brief moment and summed up our dilemma. She bent down and felt my stomach. "Well, my dear, your time is soon, isn't it?" I nodded as the sweat dripped down my face, even though the evening was cool. Joseph asked desperately, "Is there somewhere we can take shelter? I haven't much money, but my wife can't have a baby here in the street!"

She was a strong-looking woman about my mother's age. She took Joseph's hand and pulled him to his feet. "Pick up your wife and follow me, young man," she said with authority.

Joseph lifted me up with a groan and put me back on the donkey. She grabbed the donkey's reigns and began walking quickly. We walked around the inn and came to the back of the building. We approached a lovely meadow that faced rolling hills. The moon was full and there were many stars in the sky that night. There was one particular star, just above us, that sent out a brilliant light. Joseph had no trouble walking up the stone-strewn hill because of the brilliance of the night sky.

The woman, who introduced herself as Hannah, continued to talk, "You must forgive my husband for his rough manner. He has been up since early morning and has been welcoming strangers to our inn for several days. He is tired and cranky, and I'm sure he will feel bad about the way he treated you when he wakes up in the morning."

She led us to a cave toward the top of one of the hills. It was quiet there, away from the city noises. It was full of animals: donkeys, cows, sheep, and a few dogs. It must have been the place where the innkeeper allowed his visitors to keep their livestock. They had all been bedded down for the night and were peacefully watching us as we entered.

The woman went to the back of the cave and came toward me with an armload of fresh straw. Joseph lifted me from the donkey and put me down gently, as I groaned with a new pain. Hannah took a blanket off our donkey and spread it out on the bed of straw. Joseph helped me to lie down on the blanket.

She began going through our bags to see what supplies we had. "It looks like you are out of water and food. Do you have anything to use to wrap the baby when he comes?" I groaned again and shook my head no. Joseph stood still, drained of all energy and overwhelmed with worry. Neither of us had thought the baby would come this early.

Hannah sighed and said, "Stay with your wife, and I will go back to the inn for supplies. You should try to get some rest, young man. You look about as white as one of these sheep, and I daresay it will be a long night for you." She laughed quietly as she walked out of the cave, shaking her head at the foolishness of a man who would travel with a wife so large with child.

Joseph lay down beside me just as my belly tightened again. I tried not to call out, but it hurt so much. Joseph looked around for the woman and began to panic. "I'm so sorry. Did I hurt you?"

I could not speak. I just grabbed his hand, squeezed it, and shook my head back and forth. When the pain subsided, I gasped, "Joseph, the baby is here. I can feel him wanting to come out."

He was frantic. He ran to the opening in the cave and saw the woman waddling slowly toward the inn. "I'll be right back," he called to me. Before I could ask him not to leave, he was out the cave and running down the hill.

Later, we laughed as he told me how he ran, tripped, fell, and rolled down that hill in his hurry to get Hannah to move faster. He almost knocked the dear woman down as he came up to her. He grabbed her arm and ushered her into the inn. "Don't pull on me, young man. I will get there as quickly as my old bones will carry me."

"Here," she said as she handed him a jug of water, a flask of wine and a basket of food. "You carry these, and I'll carry the blankets and swaddling."

While I waited, alone, I called out to my mother, Anna. I knew she couldn't hear me, but I missed her so much. I wanted her to hold me and tell me everything was going to be fine. She was always my rock. Now, I was alone with my new husband in a faraway village filled with strangers. I loved Joseph, but he was not much help in this situation. I wanted my mother!

To distract myself, I began looking around the cave. The floor was muddy except for where patches of straw had been thrown. On one wall, where the animals seemed to cluster, there was a hollowed out section with a stone trough. This was filled with straw for the animals to eat. Next to that was a stone shelf set into the wall about knee high. Hannah had left a lantern on that shelf before she left.

On another side of the cave was a stone circle with charred bits of wood on the floor. There were other pieces of wood already cut up outside the circle. There was a spit over the fire with a bowl that was wiped clean, probably by some hungry animal. I surmised that shepherds used this cave regularly for shelter when the weather was harsh.

The animals moved about freely, but they could not leave the cave, as there was a crude gate at the opening. I was grateful for the animals, as their bodies provided some warmth. At that time of year, the evenings were cold, especially in the hilly country. As I waited for Joseph's return, one of the little lambs came up to me and nuzzled my face. I stroked its soft coat as I felt another pain coming fast.

It seemed like a very long time before Joseph and Hannah returned, although it was probably not long at all. When Joseph rushed back to me, he was perspiring and breathing heavily. The woman was several minutes behind him, but they were both back, praise the Lord!

I could not speak, the pains were so frequent and intense. I just grabbed Joseph's hand as the woman began pushing my clothes out of the way. She adjusted my legs and helped me to sit up a bit as I had seen Elizabeth do. She announced, "I see a head! We got here just in time. Now, I want you to push hard for me when I count to three." I pushed and pushed, but nothing happened. "Is this your first child, my dear?"

I couldn't answer, but Joseph answered for me. "Yes. Please help us. This child must live. Please help us."

The woman spoke gently to us. "Now, don't worry. I've delivered many babies. This one is just a little stuck, but we will get him out. You are a tiny young lady, and your first baby will take a bit more time."

I felt as if my body was splitting in two, the pain was so great. All through that time, Joseph never left my side. He prayed, held me tenderly, stroked my arm, wiped my face, and spoke loving words. The woman began to build a small fire and heat some water. Then she held a knife in the flames under the pot, as Joseph and I prayed.

At one point, when I was in the most pain, God showed me a vision of the sky filled with thousands of stars. Then, as I watched, the stars turned into angels, all singing, "Glory to God in the highest, and on earth peace to those on whom His favor rests." As I listened to the heavenly voices, my precious baby was born, and I heard his cry for the first time.

Joseph had never been in the same room when a baby was born. When he glanced down at how much blood covered my legs, the blanket, and the wriggling baby, he began to panic. "Is she all right? Is the baby harmed?"

"No, my dear," Hannah answered evenly. "There is always a lot of blood. Your wife and child are fine." Then she cut the cord with the knife, turned Jesus upside down, and gave his back a gentle slap. Jesus began to cry as breath entered his lungs. She handed Jesus to Joseph as she ordered, "You wash the baby, while I take care of your wife."

Joseph held Jesus tightly as his little body was wiggling and covered with slippery blood and mucus. Then he squatted on the earth and tenderly laid the child in his lap, as he soaked a cloth in the bowl of warm water the woman had prepared. He gently washed the blood from my son's body, and Jesus stopped crying and looked at Joseph.

I watched as Joseph's large, calloused hands tenderly stroked my baby's cheek. Tears were streaming over Joseph's face. They were tears of joy, wonder, relief, and love. He kept saying, "He's so beautiful; he's so beautiful."

I called out, "Is he all right? Does he have all of his fingers and toes and everything?"

Joseph responded, "Oh, yes. He is perfect."

Mary paused and looked at Luke and Barnabas, "Years later, I held my bloody son's body in my lap, just as Joseph had that night. I also wiped the blood from every inch of his body, but his body was not perfect then, and my tears were not tears of joy." Luke bent over and kissed the hand that had washed his Savior. Mary continued.

When Hannah had finished washing me, she covered me with a blanket. Then she went over to the fire to cook some food for us.

I put out my arms for my son. Joseph handed him to me tenderly. Jesus grabbed my finger and looked into my eyes as I sang a song to him. I looked over his tiny body. He was perfect in every way. He had soft brown eyes that seemed to take up half his face. His hair was brown and curly, and he had the cutest little feet I have ever seen. I couldn't stop kissing his feet! Joseph was sitting beside me with his arm around my shoulders and stoking our child with his other hand. He kept saying over and over, "He is so beautiful; he is so beautiful." And indeed he was—the most beautiful of all babies."

Luke looked at Mary. She had crossed her arms as if she were cradling her baby once again. Tears were streaming down her worn face as she remembered her joy that day.

Mary took a sip of water and said, "Did I ever tell you how Zachariah died?"

"No, Mother, I don't think you ever did," Barnabas said. Luke nodded. "Please tell us, Mother."

"Well, I'm sure I told you that when the wise men returned to their lands by a different route to avoid Herod, the king was very angry. He sent out his soldiers to kill all male babies under the age of two that lived anywhere near Bethlehem.

"Yes, Mother," Barnabas said, "I know that you and Joseph escaped to Egypt to save Jesus, but how did John survive?"

Elizabeth and Zachariah's village was in the path of the soldiers' slaughter. They had received word that the soldiers were on their way. John was a very active eight month-old baby by then, and almost everyone in the small village had seen him. Zachariah was an important man in the region, and the unusual birth to a barren, old woman was something everyone talked about, even beyond the borders of Jutta.

The day after Joseph and I left for Egypt, a messenger visited Elizabeth. He had been sent by one of Zachariah's friends who worked in the temple in Jerusalem. He knew the soldiers had been ordered to kill all of the baby boys in the region. The messenger had run most of the way and had managed to give warning to several parents in his path. Elizabeth and Zachariah were much too old to travel across a desert and start a new life, as Joseph and I could do. They did the only thing that could be done.

Elizabeth gave John something to drink that made him sleep. Then she and Sarah took turns carrying the baby, hidden in a basket and covered by sheep skins, as they climbed the steep hill to the summer home. They were careful to walk among the trees and bushes and away from the path.

Zachariah stayed below, waiting in their larger home at the foot of the hill. When two soldiers arrived at Ein Kerem, they pushed past Zachariah in search of the baby. They became enraged when they could not find him. They had been told by several villagers that there was a boy infant in that home. They told Zachariah that they would kill him if he did not tell them where the baby was hiding.

They tried torture first. They burned him with hot coals on his bare chest. The only words Zachariah uttered were his prayers to God for strength. Finally, they ran a sword through his heart.

One of the soldiers grabbed a servant cowering in a corner of the room and demanded to know where the baby was. They promised to torture and kill him if he did not tell them the truth. The terrified servant, who had witnessed everything they had done to his master, pointed to the hill behind the house. The soldiers raced up the hill.

When Elizabeth and her maid reached the top, Elizabeth wrapped the baby tightly in the sheep skins and placed him in the hollow at the back of the cave. The two old women used all of their strength to push a large stone against the back wall of the cave, making sure there was enough air for the baby to breathe. Just as they sat down, the soldiers arrived panting from their climb.

The rage they had felt with Zachariah had dissipated with exhaustion by the time they reached the top. They looked around but could find nothing but two old women resting by a rock in a cave home. The soldiers were tired and hungry and gave up their search quickly. They agreed to report to their centurion that they had found and killed an old man rumored to be the father of an infant. After seeing his old wife and finding no infant, they believed they had been deceived by the villagers. The centurion listened to the report and decided that his soldiers had done their job and marched his regiment to the next region to continue the slaughter.

Elizabeth took the sleeping baby out from behind the rock and held him tightly as she listened to the wailing of the women below. An hour later, John began stirring, and they determined it was safe to descend the hill. They found Zachariah's body being washed for burial by the house servants. The man that had told the soldiers to go up the hill had fled in shame. The others told Elizabeth of Zachariah's sacrifice to save John's life. I have been told that the people of the town today venerate the rock that saved John's life."

Mary paused for a sip of water. "The Roman soldiers could be cruel, but they did not know what they were doing. The light of my son had not yet reached them."

Luke said, "It is late, and we need to sleep." Mary protested. She wanted to wash and mend Barnabas' clothes before retiring.

Barnabas said, "They will keep until tomorrow, dear Mother." Luke helped her to lie down, covered her with a blanket, and gave her three kisses; one on the forehead and one on each cheek, as she had kissed him often when he was a little boy. Barnabas gave her one of his special hugs and then three kisses as well.

The men lay on their blankets by the door, talking quietly about the next few days. "I must leave soon to help Paul. The Romans can be so cruel. They may kill him if he remains in jail. Since I am not a Jew,

I may be able to arrange for his release. Let us begin preparing for the journey tomorrow so that as soon as John returns, we can leave."

Mary heard these words. Her ears were still keen. She felt sad, again, that she was such a burden to these men. She said a quick prayer to the Father to take her to his kingdom soon so these brave men could continue to spread her son's message without wasting time on her.

CHAPTER FIVE

A BOY BECOMES A MAN

The next morning, Mary rose early, carefully stepped over the sleeping men, and went outside to light the fire under the large cauldron. The sun was rising over the hills on the other side of the valley, and the earth seemed to glow with an orange sheen.

Mary stopped for a moment and said a prayer of praise to the Father for the gift of the beautiful sunrise. The air smelled sweet and clean, and the breezes were cool. There were still drops of dew on the wildflowers that grew nearby. She continued her internal prayer as she walked over to an especially beautiful bunch of red flowers and smelled their fragrance. As she finished her prayer, she walked back to the fire pit and began placing larger pieces of wood onto the pile of smaller dried brush and sticks.

Then she went into the hut for her flint stones in the small box beside the door. As she was moving about, Barnabas rolled over, sat up, and rubbed his face and beard vigorously. "Let me help you, Mother. What can I do?" he asked with a yawn. Mary pointed to the corner. "I would be most pleased if you would carry that heavy jug of water outside and pour it into the cauldron. Then go down the hill to the well and refill it for me."

"Yes, Mother," Barnabas said as he stood up quickly and stretched his arms to the ceiling. He yawned again and picked up the large jug without effort. He was strong and agile, even though he was a man in his forties. He walked outside and emptied the jug into the cauldron. Mary was stooping underneath his reach and creating sparks with her flint. "Before you head down the hill," Mary said without looking up, "go inside and take off your clothes and search my chest for a clean robe. Then put your dirty cloak and robe in this water. I will wash your things as you go for more water. Take a few coins from the chest and buy us some bread for breakfast and some flour and oil while you are in town. I plan to bake some bread later today. You and Luke will need some loaves for your journey to Caesarea."

Luke awoke as Barnabas was changing his clothes and went outside to help Mary build the fire for the wash. After putting his clothes in the cauldron, Barnabas headed down the hill wearing the clean robe he had found. It only came down to his knees and was very tight around his middle, but it served its purpose.

"Luke, let's wash your clothes as well. I think I may have another clean robe in that chest. Put it on and bring all of your dirty clothes to me." Luke came back out wearing a clean robe and carrying a handful of dirty clothes. He put them into the cauldron and took the large wooden paddle from Mary. He stirred the clothes as the water began to boil. Mary went back into the hut to roll up the sleeping mats and blankets and prepare for their morning meal.

After several minutes of stirring, Luke began taking the clothes out one by one and draping them on the nearby tree branches. He was just about done when Barnabas returned with a full jug of clean water and packages of flour, oil, fruit, and bread.

As Luke, Barnabas, and Mary sat around the small table eating their flatbread and fruit, Luke said, "Mother Mary, will you tell us the story of when the boy Jesus was missing for three days? I have often wondered how such a good, obedient son could have caused you so much worry. I know Jesus loved you very much. It just doesn't make sense to me that he would not tell you where he was going."

Mary stretched and took another date.

"Well, my son, it took me some time to understand that myself."

After the Passover feasts were over and we were preparing to leave Jerusalem with a large group of people heading north, I told Jesus to fill our jugs with water and then join Joseph and the other men as they traveled. At his age, most boys traveled with the men, but he was small and could have been in either group. As it was, Joseph assumed he was with me and the other women and children. It was not until nightfall, when Joseph and I met at the end of the day, that we realized Jesus was missing.

Even though it was total darkness and dangerous to travel, we started back toward Jerusalem immediately. We were distraught with worry, thinking about where Jesus could be and how frightened he must be. We thought perhaps he had been taken by a group of slave traders or was lost and huddled in some cold alley, hungry and frightened.

After several hours of walking, we had to stop and rest our animal. Joseph built a small fire, and we ate enough to keep up our strength.

*Before full light, we started toward Jerusalem again as fast as we could walk. Those three days we searched for Jesus were agony for us. Joseph kept blaming himself. He thought he had failed as a father. He felt the burden of not only losing our son, but losing the **Son of God**. We didn't sleep and barely took time to eat.*

It finally occurred to me to go to the home of one of my relatives, Seraphia, who lived in Jerusalem. As soon as she saw me, she knew how worried I was. She told us Jesus was well and was in the temple. We nearly ran all of the way there.

Joseph went into the temple alone, as women were not permitted to go beyond a certain point inside. I paced at the top of the steps just outside the heavy doors. It seemed a very long time before Jesus and Joseph walked out into the sunlight. I had to hold onto the wall to keep from collapsing; my legs were shaking so badly. When Jesus approached me, all I could do was hold him tightly. As I held him, it struck me how much Jesus had grown. We were nearly the same height. When I finally let go, I asked, "Son, why have you done this to us? Your father and I have been looking for you with great anxiety."

He seemed puzzled by my question. He asked me, "Why were you looking for me? Did you not know that I must be in my Father's house?" I was puzzled, and words failed me.

Joseph never spoke a word. He just put his arm around Jesus' shoulder and walked him quickly away from the crowd at the base of the steps to a place where we could be alone. He was too upset to even talk to Jesus, but I noticed tears welling in his eyes. Joseph led us to the shade of a sycamore tree where we had tied our animal. I spread a blanket in the shade, and we all sat down. At that point, I could no longer contain my emotions. I had held so much worry inside for three long days and nights that I burst into tears of relief and exhaustion. I cried for a very long time as Joseph held me tightly with one arm, keeping his other arm, just as tightly, around Jesus.

When I stopped crying, Joseph untied our animal, and we walked toward the nearest well. We all took a long drink from the cool water and refilled our jugs. Then we walked slowly and silently out of the north gate of Jerusalem and followed the road to Nazareth.

As we traveled back toward Nazareth after those three terrible days and nights of searching, I didn't take my eyes from Jesus. I slept close to him each night and reached out as he slept to just touch his shoulder or stroke his hair. I had to reassure myself that he was safe. I'm sure it was hard for a boy of his age to have his mother acting in such a way, but Jesus never protested. It took me a long time to get over my fear that he might disappear again.

As we sat by the fire the first night of our return journey, I asked Jesus again why he had done this to us. Jesus explained to Joseph and me that the day we left Jerusalem, when I had sent him off to the well to fill our jugs with water for the trip home, he had passed by the temple.

He felt a deep need to go in one last time and pray to his Father, the Lord God. So he put the empty jugs outside the temple and asked one of the beggars to find me and tell me where he was. Jesus was such a trusting boy! He was so very beautiful and always saw the good in others. That's why I was worried he had been captured by slave traders. He would have been a very valuable slave for someone. He was intelligent, healthy, and so trusting!

Mary paused with the memory of her young son. A broad smile covered her face as she pictured him in her mind. "Luke, do you think you could paint a picture of him some day as he looked back then?"

"Of course, I could, Mother," Luke answered with a smile. "You have described him so well to me over the years, I have a clear image of the young Jesus in my mind."

"That would be wonderful," Mary said, patting his knee. "Before continuing my story, I need to get the bread started." She stood up and stretched and walked over to the shelf to take down the flour, oil, yeast, and salt. As she mixed her ingredients and kneaded the dough, the men went outside to gather more wood for the fire pit. She set the dough to rise in the sunshine and called the men over to the shade of a large tree so they could enjoy the breezes of mid-afternoon on the hillside as she continued her story.

Jesus told us that as he entered the temple and came closer to the curtain that led to the Holiest of Holies, he felt as if he had arrived home. He said he knelt on the stone floor before the curtain and fell face forward with his arms and legs outstretched. As he prayed, the Holy Spirit came upon him. He was filled with more knowledge than we can imagine. He realized his destiny. He knew for the first time that he would never marry. He knew for the first time that he would spend a part of his life teaching others about his Father's kingdom. And he knew for the first time that he would suffer horribly before his life ended at an early age.

Jesus changed from a curious boy to a mature young man in those moments with the Holy Spirit, just as I had changed from a girl to a young woman when the Holy Spirit filled me with his love. It is hard to explain how we were transformed in those moments, but it changed my life completely, as it changed Jesus' life.

Barnabas spoke up softly. "I felt a dramatic transformation when the Holy Spirit came upon me," he said. "Before that, I was confused about what to do with my life. I was afraid to teach about the kingdom and the way to salvation. I worried about material things and never gave a thought to life after death. When I was consumed by the Holy Spirit, I changed completely. I am at peace with my life now. I don't always have enough food to fill my belly, and I don't always have a warm place to sleep, and sometimes I am arrested and beaten …" He paused to rub his shoulder. "But my life is better, knowing I am following the Holy Will of the Father and will one day live in His kingdom. Jesus said that his Father's kingdom has many mansions, and I am hoping mine has a big kitchen with a warm fire."

They all laughed at this. He continued, "Jesus also said not to worry about tomorrow or the clothes we wear or the food we eat. Since I stopped worrying about these things, my life is so much more peaceful and filled with joy."

Barnabas paused, stood up, turned around, and patted his stomach. They all laughed at the tight-fitting robe. "I used to be vain and bothered by such things," Barnabas said, laughing, "but now I take what comes with joy."

Luke nodded his head, smiling. "I have also been changed by the Holy Spirit."

"Of course you have, dear one," Mary said as she stroked Luke's face. "Then perhaps you will understand a little better about Jesus' behavior that day."

While Jesus was lying face down on the floor before the curtain, one of the high priests came to him and, thinking the boy had fainted, helped him rise. When Jesus stood up, the priest saw my son's beautiful face and bright glowing eyes and knew he was in the presence of a young man close to God. As they walked to a bench, Jesus began talking in a way twelve-year-old boys never talk. He began praising our heavenly Father with a beautiful prayer and with more fervor than the old priest had ever witnessed. As other priests and scholars gathered, they too were amazed.

Jesus said the hours flew by, and he didn't even think about Joseph and me until after dark when he realized how hungry he was. One of the priests who knew our family took Jesus home for nourishing food and a place to sleep.

The priest's wife, Seraphia, was a distant cousin of mine and close to my age. Seraphia's father had been a high priest as well. She was descended from Abraham and was a very holy woman. When I was a small girl, I stayed with Seraphia and her family when my parents and I visited Jerusalem for the Passover. After Jesus was born, Joseph and I stayed in her home while we participated in the purification rights at the temple in Jerusalem. Her husband bought the turtle doves for our offering as his gift for our son's birth. They were always kind to my family.

Years later, that same wonderful woman offered my son some relief as he carried his cross past her doorway. While the guards were distracted, trying to find someone in the crowd strong enough to help my son carry his cross, Jesus sat on the ground, exhausted. Seraphia came over to him silently with a bit of water. She noticed the blood from his head streaming into his eyes, so she offered Jesus her veil. After wiping his face, she offered him a sip of water. One of the guards noticed her then and cruelly grabbed the gourd and drank from it before Jesus could touch his lips to it. Then the guard pushed Seraphia away roughly and threw the gourd at her. The next day as we mourned the death of my son, that kind woman came to me and showed me her veil. My son had left an impression of his wounded face upon it to help her and others remember his suffering that day.

"I'm sorry. I have wandered away from my story about Jesus as a young boy. Please forgive me. I am an old woman, and sometimes my memory goes where it wants." The two men looked at her lovingly, not bothered at all by the shift in the story. Mary sighed deeply and continued.

After that first night with Seraphia and her husband, Jesus went back and forth between the temple and their house. He loved being close to his heavenly Father, and he loved to talk to the priests and teachers in the temple. Jesus was not really worried about us. He thought that we knew where he was. Seraphia was concerned for me. She knew how worried I must be, but what could she do? She didn't know where I was or how to tell me that my son was safe. She inquired among her friends if they knew where Joseph and I were. She was told we had left for Nazareth, but she did not tell this to Jesus.

All that time, Jesus was at peace. He needed those three days to be alone with the Holy Spirit and to fully understand his mission on earth. He thought I knew where he was and had just left him alone to be with his heavenly Father and the scholars in the temple. He never imagined that we were wandering the countryside, the desert, and the streets of Jerusalem searching for him. He thought we knew he was safe and well cared for. He never meant to cause us any anxiety.

Jesus apologized many times as we traveled the long way back to Nazareth, and so he put up with my over-protectiveness. He knew it caused me anxiety if he went anywhere alone. I had nightmares about Jesus being lost or captured and put in chains for many years. I'm sure Satan was the cause of these dreams. I had to pray constantly for God to give me peace.

Mary paused in her story and looked at Luke. "I had been praying for three days to find my son safe. Every time we came near a bend in the road or turned down an alley, I would pray that we would find Jesus there. God did not answer my prayer the way I wanted, but in His way and in His time. You know, Luke, our Father always listens to our prayers, but sometimes He knows a better solution or time than we desire. We just need to trust in Him and let go of our worry. Paul knows this. Paul has great faith. When you go to him, it will be at the time God has planned. So don't worry so much."

At this, she squeezed Luke's hand. Luke shook his head and then laid it on Mary's shoulder. "Yes, Mother, I have much to learn from you. Please continue your story."

A week after we returned home, I felt silly about being so protective, so I put my trust in God and sent Jesus to fetch water from the well at the center of our small village. When Jesus came home from gathering the water, I could see that he was very upset. I asked him what was wrong, and he told me that he had met Rachel at the well.

Rachel was a pretty young girl about Jesus' age. They had known each other since we returned from Egypt. They had played together often, and the women of the town began nodding to one another as they saw them together. Many thought that Jesus and Rachel would one day be married. Jesus liked Rachel very much, and as they grew older, it was amusing to watch their relationship change.

Rachel's father had talked to Joseph about a betrothal a year earlier. Joseph suggested that they wait a few more years before settling the matter. He did not know if the Savior was destined to marry or not, and he needed more time for God to reveal His plan to us.

Rachel was developing into a young woman, and over that season she and Jesus stopped playing together and became shy around one another. They, of course, were aware of the talk among their families and friends. They weren't sure how to handle their maturing feelings.

After Jesus' experience in the temple, He was no longer a playful youth; he was a man. He hadn't changed physically, but those close to him saw a remarkable change in his demeanor and behavior. He knew his future was no longer going to be with a wife and family.

When Jesus met Rachel that day at the well, she was friendly to him in her shy way. She had no way of knowing that his goals for the future had changed. Jesus didn't know how to tell her. He filled his water jar and walked away quickly. He knew he had offended her by not returning her smile or saying hello, but he wasn't sure how to deal with her. His heart ached, and he was so young.

He was sad that he couldn't have a life with her or any other woman. It was difficult for him to explain his feelings to me when he returned home. As he struggled to tell me, he began to cry. The words poured out of him. He wanted a normal, simple life. He wanted to have a wife and children and to live to see his grandchildren. But he knew God's Will for him was something different. He knew that doing the Father's Will was the only way to true joy and salvation for all mankind. He was learning that the path God wants us to take is usually the most difficult path of all.

He was still young enough to cry in his mother's arms, but mature enough to realize that his course was set. He had said yes to the Father that day in the temple, just as I had said yes thirteen years before that.

He washed his face, kissed me on the cheek, and took my hand. We prayed to the Father for the courage to continue to follow His holy will.

After our prayer, Jesus took a deep breath, kissed me one more time, and took a gourd of cool water outside to where Joseph was working.

I watched them talk for some time. Jesus explained that Joseph would have to talk to Rachel's father about Jesus' call to celibacy. Joseph nodded, not fully understanding, but accepting God's will once again. He took a long sip of water and handed the piece of wood he had been sanding to Jesus. Then Joseph walked out to find Rachel's father. When Joseph returned, he and Jesus worked together in silence until I called them to wash up for the evening meal.

I never saw Jesus cry again until years later when Joseph died.

In a few years, Rachel found another man, married, and had children, but I think she never forgot her first love.

Mary finished her story with a smile. Luke and Barnabas sat still as they gazed upon her beautiful face. They were in awe of her great faith. They joined hands as Mary said, "My little ones, you must pray without ceasing. Pray from your hearts. Pray to Jesus. Talk to him. Surrender your Wills to the Father. Let Jesus become your constant companion. He will bear you up and carry your burdens. Without prayer, you can never hope to conquer Satan."

After a bit of silence, Luke stood up, stretched, and picked up the water jug for another trip to the well. He wanted to keep the water jugs full, in case they were called away quickly.

Barnabas stepped outside, took the dry clothes from the trees, and went back inside to change. Mary put the loaves of bread in the oven. She moved the hot embers on top and around the sides of the oven. Then she added more wood to the fire and walked back into her hut. Mary lifted her sewing basket to her lap and motioned to Barnabas to bring her the tattered cloak.

As she tended to her mending by the light of the late-afternoon sun, Barnabas changed into his own clean robe and put the borrowed robe back into the chest. Then, he walked up the hill to gather more fuel for the fire. He cleaned out the cauldron and put some fresh water in it to heat for their dinner.

Luke returned, picked some vegetables from their garden, cleaned and added them to the water. He took the loaves of bread out of the oven and put them on the table.

By then, Mary had finished her mending, and they had their meal together as the setting sun flooded the hillside with pink and yellow hues.

After eating, Mary rested on her cot, exhausted, and fell fast asleep.

The men began to quietly pack little bundles of supplies for the trip to Caesarea, in the event John should return in the next day or two. Then, they spread out their blankets as before and slept near the doorway.

CHAPTER SIX

A WINK AND A SMILE

John arrived home the next afternoon.

At the age of thirty-three, he was the youngest of the original twelve apostles and was the same age now that Jesus had been when he died. At this moment however, he looked much older. He had been sleeping out in the open for several nights and was covered with dust and grime, and he hadn't eaten a warm meal for a week. His long, brown hair was stringy, and his beard was bushy with some grey beginning to appear. His light-brown eyes, usually full of light, looked dull as they reflected the dark circles underneath. His outer cloak was filthy and torn in several places. As he came into the hut, he shed his cloak in a heap by the door and rushed to hug Mary. As they ended their embrace, Luke and Barnabas took turns welcoming their brother with hearty hugs.

John went outside with the men to wash his hands and face. As he dipped his hands in the bowl of water Barnabas brought over to him, Luke told him what had happened to Mary—her hunger and thirst and her fall. Luke also told him of his desire to leave for Caesarea as soon as possible to help Paul.

While the men were outside, Mary prepared a meal with all of the remaining food in the hut. There was a big bowl of warm gravy for dipping the bread she had baked yesterday, three kinds of fruit, and a bowl of nuts.

With sad eyes, John entered the hut, gave Mary another tender hug, and sat down. Before he could speak an apology, Mary patted his hand and said, "I am fine. I have a few cuts and a swollen knee. But it is nothing. Now enjoy your meal."

All four of them sat around the table, held hands, and prayed in thanksgiving for John's safe return. They asked God to protect Peter and Paul and all others traveling in the name of Jesus. Then they enjoyed the hearty meal and one another's company.

While they ate, John explained that he had been able to find Mark a few days' travel from Rome. Mark had promised to find Peter and arrange for his release from prison, so John had headed straight back to Ephesus.

When the meal was completed, Luke and Barnabas reluctantly stood up to leave. Luke made John promise three times that he would not leave Mary alone.

Mary asked Luke and Barnabas to bow their heads as she put a hand on each in blessing.

She spoke these words in a strong voice, "It is my heart's desire that you should live your lives in great peace and joy. Too many of my children allow their fear of what the future might hold to diminish that joy and peace. My little ones, if you give your hearts completely to my son and trust in him without doubt, you have absolutely nothing to fear. If you allow fear and doubt to creep into your hearts, Satan will use that fear against you. Instead, allow your hearts to dwell on God's infinite love and grace. As children of the light, allow your hearts to leap for joy! Thanks to the precious blood of my son that was shed for you, Satan has no claim or power over you. However, if you allow fear and doubt to creep into your hearts, you are giving Satan that power to use against you. Trust in Jesus! Now go in peace to love and serve the Lord."

As she finished her blessing, Barnabas and Luke embraced their loving Mother one last time and turned around and headed up the mountain quickly in hopes of catching the same boat that had brought John across the sea.

As Mary and John sat quietly together in the fading sunlight, Mary reached over from her stool, picked up her sewing basket, and said, "John, shake your cloak outside and then hand it to me. I will mend it and then wash it for you. It looks about as haggard as you do."

John stood up and retrieved his cloak from the corner by the door where he had dropped it when coming in. He stepped outside and shook it vigorously. Little bits of leaves, sticks, and dust flew down the hillside. Mary moved her stool near the door to catch the last rays of daylight.

When John came back in, he sat quietly and watched Mary sew his torn cloak. He said a silent prayer, thanking God for the gift of this blessed woman. He had never known someone so full of grace and peace.

He broke the silence and said softly, "Mother, as I was traveling home alone, I had a lot of time to think. I was remembering how my life began changing as I witnessed Jesus' first miracle. It was also the day I first met you. Do you remember that day? I have been puzzled about something for a long time. I never understood Jesus' words to you. Do you remember what he said?"

Mary looked up from her sewing, a warm smile lighting up her face. She nodded and met his eyes.

John deepened his voice to imitate Jesus and said, "Woman, how does your concern affect me? My hour has not yet come."

Then John continued in his own voice. "Mary, you brushed off his comment as if you did not even hear it, then got up and walked over to where several servers were standing. You said, "Do whatever he tells you." That's when Jesus went over and told them to fill the empty jugs with water. After they had filled six jars as directed, Jesus laid his hand on the lip of each jar and said a blessing. Next, he told a server to draw out the contents and take it to the head waiter. The man did as Jesus asked, and the head waiter called the bridegroom over and said, 'Everyone serves the good wine first and then, after the people have drunk freely, an inferior one; but you have kept the good wine until now.' Then, they began pouring out the wine for the guests."

John paused, looked into Mary's eyes, and continued, "At that time, I was focused on the water and wine, and I was in awe of Jesus' power to perform the miracle. But later, I wondered why Jesus spoke to you that way. It seemed so—forgive me, Mother—so disrespectful. Do you remember?"

Mary smiled and said, "Oh, yes, I remember that day very well. I think of it often. In spite of what you think, we had a great deal of fun that day. It is one of my favorite memories. I was teasing Jesus, and he was teasing me right back. Didn't you notice the way he rolled his eyes at me when I turned to the servers instead of responding to him?"

John shook his head no and took her hand carefully. The bandage was still stained with blood. Mary let him hold and kiss her hand, and then she reclaimed it to continue with her sewing as she resumed her story.

As Jesus and I traveled to Cana that morning for the wedding, we were talking about our Father's Holy Will. I said that it was time for him to leave me and to tell others about the kingdom of his Father. Jesus insisted that he couldn't leave me alone just yet, since I was a widow with no one to support me. I said I could travel with him some of the time, and other times I could stay with Salome and her husband Cleophas. I told him that I would be fine. Salome and her family lived near Nazareth and had often helped us during Joseph's illness and death.

We had known since Jesus was baptized that our time together was drawing to a close. We had been planning for his departure, even before his baptism. We had been setting aside some savings for when he would no longer work as a carpenter. Even as Joseph lay dying, the three of us discussed what we could do to provide for me after Jesus left. There was a workroom full of items that could be sold when money was needed. I knew I would be fine, but Jesus was still hesitant to leave me alone. It had only been about two months since Joseph had died when we traveled to the wedding.

When I publicly told the servers to do whatever Jesus wanted them to do, I forced a decision upon him. He had no gracious way out. He could either do as I wished or leave the wedding in shame. I had out witted him! If you had been watching us carefully, instead of watching the servers and wine jars, you would have seen some eye-rolling and winking between us. I started laughing as he stood up with a shrug. He turned to me with a huge grin and reached down and gave my shoulders a squeeze and my forehead a kiss. My son knew it was time to begin his public ministry. He did as I asked, as he always did. He performed the miracle and started his public life.

"The wedding was a wonderful place for a new beginning, don't you think?" Mary asked John with a wink. He nodded yes, and she continued.

After we tasted the new wine, we had fun dancing and laughing the rest of the day. We knew it would not be long before we separated, so we enjoyed each minute we had together. We had not had so much fun since before Joseph became ill.

John put his hand on Mary's knee and said, "Mother, I did not know you when Joseph died. Can you tell me what happened?"

"Of course, my dear. But it is getting too dark to sew now, so I will finish my mending and my story in the morning."

Mary laid John's cloak on top of her basket and stood up to stretch. "Let's have a drink of water and then go to bed for the night."

"Yes, Mother. I am tired myself. It has been a very long day. Your story will keep."

John rolled out Mary's mat by the back wall. He helped Mary lie down, and he covered her with a blanket. Then he went outside and added a large piece of wood to keep the fire going until morning. He came back inside and rolled out his mat in front of the door. He preferred to sleep by the door in the summer to catch the cool breezes and for Mother Mary's safety. Anyone wanting entry would trip over his body in the dark. There were not many people here in Ephesus who wanted to harm Christians, but John had seen many followers arrested and killed in the last fifteen years. He wanted to take all the precautions he could.

They both fell asleep quickly.

As the sun began to rise the next morning, John woke up and went to the jar of water. He poured out a cup for Mary first and placed it beside her mat. Then he took a long drink and went outside to freshen up. He came back into the hut and took some coins from the chest, being careful not to disturb Mary's other treasures.

He went over to wake Mary, touched her shoulder and said, "Mother, I am going down the hill to buy us some food and get more water from the well. I will be back soon. You rest here until I return."

She patted his hand and rolled over. It was a comfort to her to have John back from his travels. She could relax knowing that he was safe and they were together.

They had always had a special connection. John was the one apostle to come to her immediately after Jesus had been arrested. He had stayed with her throughout that long night and then left with her before the sun was up the next morning to lead her to Pilate's courtyard. He had been the only man to stay with her throughout her son's passion and death. John had held her at the foot of the cross as she collapsed when Jesus died. He had helped take Jesus from the cross and had helped to prepare his body for burial. He never left her side all through the days that followed. Each night he slept just outside her room.

Now John was being called to teach others about the kingdom of God, just as her son had been called. He was just as reluctant to leave her as Jesus had been. She prayed to God for a way to allow John to do the work that was needed.

With these thoughts, she drifted off to sleep. She awoke when John walked back into the hut to prepare their morning meal. He had some cornmeal cakes, more fruit, and a bit of mutton.

Mary clapped her hands with joy. She had not had meat in many days.

"How did you come by the meat?" she asked. "I didn't think we had enough money for that."

John replied, "I encountered a shepherd along the path from town who gave it to me as a gift. He said it was for the lovely Mother on the hill."

Mary almost blushed but enjoyed the gift. "This will make a wonderful stew for our morning meal," she said. They worked together in harmony, making their breakfast.

After eating, Mary picked up her sewing once again. "Would you like to hear about Joseph's death now?"

"Yes, Mother, very much," John said as he wiped the pot clean with the last piece of his corn cake.

When Jesus was twenty-nine years old and Joseph was fifty-seven, our lives began to change. Joseph had worked hard for many years. He had always been strong, but I began to notice a change. He needed to rest often and would ask Jesus to finish the task or lift the heavy pieces of wood. His appetite went away, and he began to pick at his food. He was never a man to complain when he was hurt or ill, so he never told me that he did not feel well. He said he was only getting old, but I knew it was more than that.

In four months, I saw Joseph go from a strong man who could work many hours without stopping to a very thin, pale, weak man who could not eat or sleep peacefully. He was in a great deal of pain. In the end, Jesus and I just held his hands and prayed for his death to come swiftly, for he was suffering so much. Jesus loved Joseph deeply. They had spent so much time together over the years. They had a very special bond, and it was hard for Jesus to say good-bye.

Joseph left this life peacefully. He closed his eyes and took one last breath as we both held his hands. Jesus cried and shared with me that he was so sorry he could not spare Joseph's life. He said it was not the Father's Holy Will for him to live any longer. Jesus knew he had the gift of healing, but it was not yet time to use that gift. It broke his heart to say good-bye to his father on earth.

After Joseph was buried, Jesus was faced with a dilemma. Should he stay and take care of me as was his duty according to custom, or should he leave me to carry out his mission and begin his ministry for the Father?

Mary paused to wipe a tear from her face. "John, you are facing the same crossroads. It is time for you to leave me and follow your path. You need to be out there in the world, spreading the words of my son, not here in this hut with me. Do you understand?"

"Yes, Mother, I understand what you are saying, but I don't have a solution. I can never leave you alone again. I won't."

"Well," Mary said with a sigh, "we will put this in God's hands. We know what He wants, and if we surrender our wills to Him, it will all work out. Now, your robe is done! But it needs a good washing, as do your other clothes. I'll go outside and wash the cauldron and fill it with clean water. You can go into the chest and find something to put on while I wash all of your robes. I have some of my clothes and blankets to wash as well. You can help me stir and hang the wash to dry."

Mary hobbled over to the pile of her dirty clothes in the corner and took them outside into the sunshine as John searched in the chest for something clean to wear. As he moved objects about, he found the robe Jesus had worn the day He died. John kissed the robe and laid it reverently back into the chest, wondering what should become of it.

CHAPTER SEVEN

THE EXODUS

The next day, Ruth poked her head in the doorway as Mary was sitting down for her morning meal. As the little girl stepped into the ray of light coming through the window, Mary could see Ruth supporting her right arm with her left hand. One side of her face was swollen and bruised. Her lip had been split, and blood had dried on her chin.

Mary put her piece of bread down, pushed the table away, and said softly, "Come here, little one. Let me look at you."

The old woman had been sitting cross-legged on the floor and resting her back against one of the tapestries attached to the wall. Ruth walked over shyly and slumped into Mary's outstretched arms. She fit into the bowl formed by Mary's legs and laid her head against the old woman's breast. As Mary wrapped her arms around the child, she could feel her rib cage through her ragged robe. Mary cradled Ruth in her arms and then leaned back and stroked her short, tangled hair with one hand. Mary could feel the girl's heart pounding. She wondered if it was from the climb up the hill or from the fighting in the hut below.

Then Mary called John into the hut. He had been outside repairing the cracks in the wall. The stone hut was solid, but weather regularly eroded the spaces between the stones, and it was a constant task keeping the holes plugged.

"John, please bring a clean cloth and fill a bowl with some warm water you will find heating over the fire. I also need that jar of salve Luke keeps on the shelf over there." She pointed to a shelf in the dark corner of the hut over the chest. "Would you also please bring a goblet of cool water for Ruth to drink?"

John looked at Ruth, almost hidden in Mary's embrace, and nodded. He knew Ruth's family. Often Abigail would send her little daughter out of the house for her safety. Amos, her father, drank too much wine. He was not well-liked in the town and had trouble finding work. He took on odd jobs—harvesting crops, helping others construct their homes—anything he could get. When Amos could not find work, or when he lost a job, he would take out his frustrations on Abigail and Ruth.

John and Mary often prayed for the family, especially for the little girl; she was so small and fragile.

Mary held Ruth close as she hummed a soothing tune and rocked her until the girl's little heart slowed its pace. Then Mary tenderly washed Ruth's cut lip and applied the salve. She put a cool cloth on her bruised jaw and examined her arm. It had a nasty bruise, but it wasn't broken, so Mary wrapped it with a moist cloth and kissed her on the forehead to finish the job.

After a time, Mary let the child out of her arms and motioned for Ruth to sit by the table. "Now, sip on this water slowly, and I will get something for you to eat." Ruth took the goblet and began taking small sips. She enjoyed the feel of the cool water on her lips.

Mary got up slowly, still hampered by her swollen knee, and handed Ruth the piece of bread she had set aside on the table. She watched as the little girl tried to bite off a piece. Ruth had difficulty with the tough bread. Her jaw and lip would not allow her mouth to open wide.

Mary said softly, "Wait a few minutes, dear, until I make some warm gravy." Then she walked over to the hearth and mixed some flour and warm water with a few herbs. She spooned some of the thick juice into a bowl and handed it to Ruth. The little girl dipped the stiff bread into the gravy and took small bites until it was gone. Mary gave her the piece of hard bread she had set aside for John and watched Ruth eat that hungrily. She suspected the girl had not been fed in a while.

When Ruth handed Mary the empty bowl she shyly thanked her for the food. As Mary washed the bowl, Ruth stood up and walked outside the hut to see what John was doing. He showed her how to fill in the cracks with the paste he had made. John assigned her to the lower spaces while he patched the higher ones. Ruth began singing as she helped John fortify the back wall of the hut. She liked to feel useful. After a while, the job was done and John patted Ruth on the head. "You were a great help to me, little one."

As John's stomach growled, he ducked his head into the hut and said, "Mother, since you have someone watching over you, I will go into town for some supplies and food." From past experience, John surmised that his little helper had eaten her way through his breakfast. Mary nodded knowingly.

Ruth came back into the hut, feeling very grown up with the responsibility of caring for the kind, old woman. She sat beside Mary and asked bravely, "Mother, I know you were not born here in Ephesus. My mother told me that you lived far away once. She said that her mother knew you years ago in a town called Nazareth. Mommy said they moved here when she was a little girl to escape the high taxes and the Romans. She said that you moved here to escape your shame because you are a sinner. I don't understand what all of that means. Can you tell me why you moved to this hut on the mountain? How did you get here from a faraway place called Nazareth? Where is Nazareth?" She paused, took a long breath, and asked, "What is a sinner?"

Mary held Ruth's small hand in both of her pale hands and said, "Well, dear, you have asked me many questions. Do you have a long time to hear all of the answers? Will your mother want you home soon?"

"Oh, no!" Ruth exclaimed. "When my father started hitting us, she told me to run and hide and not come back until dark. I can stay all day if that's all right with you."

Mary stood up. "Of course, you may stay. Now, let's see. You wanted to know about Nazareth, my home before I came to this place on the mountain. Well, let me show you."

Mary took Ruth by the hand and led her outside to a place of level ground a few paces from the door. John had cleared a bit of land for a second vegetable garden last spring, but had not had a chance to plant anything.

"First, we will smooth out the dirt, and then we will draw a map here so you can see how far I have traveled." Mary picked up a hoe leaning against the wall of the house and smoothed the dirt. "Now, go over there by that tree and find a good sturdy stick with a sharp end."

Ruth scurried off and returned in a minute with a thick stick and a big smile on her face. She was a bright young girl and loved the idea of learning something new from this kind, old woman. Mary took the stick and bent over the smoothed dirt. First she drew a large oval and put wavy lines inside.

"This is the large sea on the other side of our mountain. It is very deep, and sometimes winds blow so hard they make huge waves that capsize ships."

Ruth nodded in understanding. She had heard stories about the sea but had never seen it. The farthest she had been from her home was up this hill to Mary's hut.

Next, Mary drew the sun rising. "This is where the sun rises each morning." From where they were standing, they could see some of the homes in Ephesus at the bottom of the hill. Mary pointed to the town and said, "We see the sun rise over there, past the town of Ephesus." Mary drew a circle to represent the town of Ephesus. "Turn around and you are facing the top of the mountain. That is where we see the sun set." Mary sketched a line on the east side of the large circle. "Here is our mountain. Now, go fetch several rocks of different sizes and colors and bring them back to me."

When Ruth returned with a handful of stones, Mary picked out a very small one and placed it on the east side of the long line. "Here is my hut." Then she picked out several smaller stones and put them inside the small oval northeast from her hut. "Here are the huts in Ephesus.

Even though you walked a long way to visit me, the pebbles are very close. Do you understand how my picture in the dirt represents where we live?"

Ruth nodded, but kept her eyes riveted to the developing map in front of her bare feet. She was delighted with this activity and forgot all about the troubles in her hut at the foot of the hill.

Next, Mary put a larger stone along the southeast shore line of the sea. "This is Joppa. A boat left from Joppa to take me here." Before I got on the boat, I was living here in Jerusalem." Mary put a very large stone southeast of Joppa to represent Jerusalem. "I lived in Jerusalem for ten years after my son died."

Mary then selected a small but very beautiful stone that glistened in the sun. She placed it a little southeast of Jerusalem as she continued, "And this, my child, is the small town of Bethlehem where my son Jesus was born." Mary settled herself on the ground and continued.

We did not stay there long, but it is one of my most special memories. We arrived there tired, hungry, and afraid, with no friends to help us. Many angels came to comfort us, and they sang wonderful songs. It was a most beautiful sound! There was a bright star shining that illuminated the sky. After my precious baby was born, some people came to help us. The shepherds came first. They brought us milk and cheese and bread with bits of roasted mutton for our first meal. I think it was the most delicious food I ever tasted! The shepherd's wives and children came the next morning to bring us more food, warm wool blankets, and strips of clean white wool for my baby.

Ruth saw Mary's eyes beginning to water with the memories. She squatted down and put her arms around the older woman. "I wish I could have been there. I wish I could have held your baby. I love babies. I bet he was beautiful."

Mary continued.

Yes, he was the most beautiful baby I have ever seen. Many days later, three kings came from a far-off land. They gave us gold and other precious gifts. The sale of some of those gifts helped us travel to Egypt. It provided food and shelter for us in a strange land. You see, the king had sent soldiers to find and kill all male babies in and around Bethlehem. God sent an angel to tell Joseph, my husband, that we needed to leave quickly and go into Egypt.

"Where is Egypt?" Ruth asked, jumping back up to look at their map once again, "and what is an angel?"

"One question at a time!" Mary said, laughing. She stood up slowly, stretched her back, and put a large stone on the south side of the sea. "This is Alexandria on the shore of Egypt. We had to walk here from Bethlehem. We lived there for a few years until it was safe to go home."

Mary dragged the stick from Bethlehem to Alexandria to show how far they had walked. Then she put a small rock east of Joppa. "This rock represents Nazareth. This is where I was born, where my parents were born, where your mother was born, and where Jesus grew up. This was our home."

She drew a small circle with wavy lines northeast of Nazareth. "This is the Sea of Galilee where John, Peter, Andrew, and others used to fish." Then she drew a curly line south from the sea. "And this is the Jordan River where we were baptized."

Mary spread her arms over the map. Then she sat down again slowly. She spoke more to herself than to Ruth. "I would have been content to spend the rest of my life in Nazareth … quietly, obscurely … but that was not what God wanted." Then she turned to Ruth and said, "It is much better to follow God's will than your own. Life is certainly interesting when you let God lead."

Ruth smiled and came near. "Is John your son? He calls you *Mother*."

"Well, in a way he is my son. He has lived with me for the last fifteen years. Many people call me *Mother*. Would you like to?"

"Oh, yes," Ruth said. "You are so good to me. I like to think of you as my mother … or perhaps my grandmother."

Mary laughed. "Whatever you want is fine with me. Now, what were your other questions? You had so many."

Ruth responded hesitantly. "Dear … Mother, please tell me, what is an angel? You said angels sang songs as your son was born, and an angel told Joseph to move to Egypt. I have never heard of angels. Are they Romans or Jews or pagans? Are they gods like Diana? Where do they come from? What do they look like?"

Mary laughed until her voice sounded like tinkling bells. "Well, my dear, they are not of this earth, but they are not gods. They are beings from heaven and gifts to us from the Father. They are all around us. You have a special angel here with you right now, and her job is to guard you from harm."

Ruth turned around in a circle to look for her angel.

Mary smiled as she watched the child. "We usually can't see the angels, dear, but you can talk to your angel if you like. I think your special angel brought you to my hut this morning just to cheer me up! Some angels are guardians and some are messengers. And they have names. Gabriel was the angel who visited me when I was a young girl of fourteen and who talked to Joseph. You can name your special angel. What would you like to call her?"

Ruth beamed with joy thinking about her special angel. She thought about the times she might have been hurt or lost and that maybe an angel had led her to safety. "May I call my angel 'Mary'? May I? When I cannot be with you, I would like to think that my special angel is close to me."

Mary put her arm about Ruth as she sat beside her. "Certainly you may. Then, each night before you go to sleep, talk to Mary, your special angel. Thank her for protecting you that day, and ask her to protect and guide you the next day."

"I will!" shouted Ruth with excitement. "And now, please tell me … why does my mother call you a sinner? What is a sinner?"

Mary looked down the hillside in sorrow. "That is hard for you to understand now. Perhaps when you are older, your mother can tell you more about what she believes."

Ruth looked disappointed, but trusted Mary to know best. She nodded and said, "Tell me more about how you came to Ephesus."

Mary squeezed Ruth's shoulder as the girl settled into her lap. She leaned against the outside wall of the hut and began.

I stayed in Jerusalem after Jesus died because most of his followers were there. We were like a very large family, and I was their mother. It was a big job! God wanted me to stay with them as long as they needed me.

After some time, Jerusalem became a dangerous place for those who followed my son. You see, Ruth, some people in power were threatened by what men like John were preaching. Many people who continued teaching about Jesus were put in chains. Some were tortured, and some were killed. A man of great faith named Stephen was stoned to death outside one of the gates of Jerusalem for teaching about my son. When that happened, John became afraid for me. He felt responsible for my safety, so he and Luke began talking about where I could live.

John had been to Ephesus a few years earlier to establish a church. Luke and Paul had also been to Ephesus and had friends there. Christians felt safe in Ephesus, so John decided to bring me here. When James, the elder, was killed, John said we could delay no longer. Luke went to Joppa and bought passage on a ship to take the three of us to the shore on the other side of this mountain. John and I followed when we got word from Luke that he had found a ship. A few days later, I was on a boat with John and Luke headed for this land.

I had never been on a large boat before. I was frightened and unsteady on my feet. It was cold on the ship, and I was not able to sleep well. John and Luke were very protective of me and tried to coax me to eat, but the rolling waves made me too sick.

We had been given a very small space to keep our things, and my chest took up most of that space. It left only enough space for one person, so John and Luke insisted I sleep there. I think the men slept on the top deck when they could.

Our second day out, the sky became dark, and the wind began to blow. Thunder crashed and lightning began to light up the sky. The rain came down in torrents. Many brave men were frightened. The boat took on a great deal of water, and we were all soaked to the skin.

John tied me to a beam below, so I would not be knocked about and bruised. Then he wrapped his body around mine to protect me from injury, as things began falling all around us. At the height of the storm, I saw two men coming down the ladder and taking large items up to the surface. They were tossing them overboard to lighten the ship. On their next trip down the ladder, they began to untie my chest. John and I begged them to leave it, but they could not be convinced of its value.

I began to pray at the top of my voice to God to calm the storm and save my chest, as it contained many items of special value to our community of Christians. At that instant, the storm stopped. The men had been half-way up the ladder with my chest when the movement of the boat halted and the sun came out. They looked at one another, then at me, and quickly returned my chest to its space. I began praising God for His goodness and power.

A few hours later, those two men talked to John and were baptized by him on the ship. The Father saved my chest because it contains relics of incredible value, worth more than all the gold in the world.

"What does the chest contain that is so important?" Ruth asked as she stood up and walked into the hut.

Mary stood up, brushed the dirt from her gown and followed Ruth into the hut.

"Open the lid, and we will see," Mary said quietly.

The hinges creaked as Ruth opened it slowly. Mary helped her push the lid all the way back and reached in and took out a small painting of Jesus praying. She handed it to Ruth tenderly. "Here. Luke painted this." Ruth looked at it a long time. "He looks so"—she searched for a word—"good," she finally said.

"Yes, my dear," Mary said quietly. "He is very good."

Then Mary took out a length of cream-colored cloth the size of a woman's veil. As she unfolded it carefully, the image of a face became visible to Ruth.

"Is this your son too?" Ruth asked. Mary nodded. "He looks sad. What is that around his head?"

Mary almost whispered. "It is a cruel crown of thorns meant to mock and torture my son. He endured much pain for all mankind. He also did this for you, Ruth … for you, your Mother, and your father. Jesus endured this pain and humiliation to erase the sins people commit and to allow all of us to enter into his heavenly kingdom."

Ruth remembered Mary's stories of heaven.

Suddenly, Mary had an idea. "You should take this home and show your mother and father. Tell them about my son and how much he loves them. Tell them all that he suffered so that they can have eternal life with him in heaven."

Mary put the veil into Ruth's hands, and the little girl held it reverently. "Oh, Mother, I will do all that you ask. Do you have something we can wrap it in so it will not get dirty on the way home?"

Mary pulled out a small blanket. "Here, I won't need this, now that it is warm. Let's wrap it up to protect it." Mary laid the blanket on the table and then Ruth laid the veil on top. Mary carefully wrapped the blanket around it, then reached into her tinder box by the door and pulled out a small piece of rope. "We can tie it all together so it will stay nice and safe."

Mary left the bundle on the table and went back to the chest, put the painting back inside, and closed the lid. We can examine the contents of the chest another time. I am suddenly tired." She sat on the stool by the table. "Come, I will finish my story."

Ruth sat beside Mary but kept her eyes on the precious bundle on the table. Mary continued.

Our ship had sustained some damage from the storm, so we sailed into the nearest port for repairs. I was so happy to leave the ship for a few days. John found a small room for us in the town of Cyprus. At last I could take a walk and eat without getting sick. Shortly, however, the boat was repaired, and we were back on board. The ship headed straight for the port near Ephesus, and we arrived the next morning.

When we landed on shore, Tychicus, a friend of Paul, met us with two donkeys and a few strong men. The men insisted that I ride one of the donkeys over the mountain. The other one was used to carry most of our belongings. Four men had to carry my chest, as the path to Ephesus was too narrow and uneven for a cart. Before sundown, we were over the mountain and in the home of Aquila and Priscilla. They had emigrated from Corinth and knew Luke and Paul. We stayed with them until John and Luke built this hut.

Ephesus is a wonderful community where Jews, Gentiles, and pagans live together in harmony, respect, and tolerance. I'm glad we came here … especially since it gave me a chance to meet you!

Mary gave Ruth a gentle pat and looked to the door as she heard someone coming.

John ducked his head and entered the hut with his arms full. He had a large bag bulging and another large jug of fresh water. He put the jug down beside the door and the bag on the table. Then he shed his cloak and hung it on a peg just inside the door. As he turned back to the table to unload the bag of food, he noticed the bundle. "What do we have here?" he asked.

Mary explained what it was and that she had suggested Ruth take it to her parents. John was worried about trusting such a precious relic to a small girl and her pagan parents, but he yielded to Mary's judgment. John knew from experience not to question Mary's decisions. She was filled with the Holy Spirit and always knew the right thing to do.

They happily shared a meal of raisins, bread, and figs as the setting sun rested on the mountain top.

"Before it gets dark, dear, you should head home. I don't want you to fall on your way down the hill, and I don't want your mother to worry."

Ruth kissed Mary on the forehead as she reluctantly stood up. Mary reached for Ruth and took the girl's face in her old, rough hands. She gave her three kisses: one on the forehead and one on each cheek. Then she put the bundle into the girl's arms.

"I will take good care of it," Ruth promised solemnly.

"I know you will," Mary said with one more kiss on her forehead.

John stood outside and watched as Ruth made her way down the hill with the bundle under her arm. When she was out of sight, he came back into the hut.

"It's a shame we can't let her live here," he said as he walked toward Mary. "I hate sending her back to those parents with so much darkness in their hearts."

"Well, let's pray for them all," said Mary resolutely. "We will ask God to send His Spirit to them so they see what a precious child they have and learn to love her as they should."

As the light began to fade, the old woman and John knelt together on their mats and prayed fervently for Ruth and her parents, Abigail and Amos.

CHAPTER EIGHT

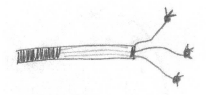

THE TEMPTATION

The next morning, John and Mary sat on their mats, praying for Ruth, her family, and their extended family traveling in faraway lands.

As they finished the prayer, Priscilla ducked her head and entered the hut. Priscilla and her husband, Aquila, had immigrated to Ephesus from Greece after their conversion by Paul. Aquila was a well-established cloth merchant, respected by many for his honest transactions. They were a well-to-do couple in their forties who had great faith in the Lord. They felt called to use their good fortune in caring for the mother of Jesus and the little community of Christians in Ephesus. For the last few months, Priscilla and her husband had been traveling to buy and sell their bolts of cloth and to spend time with their family in Corinth.

Priscilla's arms were laden with fresh fruit, a leg of lamb, flour, and oil. She put these on the table and then dug into her pocket and handed John a bag of coins. She also brought news of Andrew. She said that he was well and had been preaching in Corinth and had requested that John join him as soon as possible. When Priscilla said this, Mary looked at John, and John looked away. John was not ready to leave Mary alone or even discuss it.

John busied himself by putting the fruit in the bowl, the flour and oil on a shelf, and the coins in the chest, without a word to Priscilla.

Then he announced that he would go out to gather wood for the fire to cook the lamb.

Priscilla wisely guessed that this was a sensitive subject and turned to Mary. She took her hands, bowed her head, and asked for Mary's blessing. Then she went outside to put the lamb on the spit. John had already returned with the wood and was building up a nice fire. He stayed outside, and Priscilla went back into the hut to be with Mary.

The two women sat together on Mary's mat, arm in arm, talking of the events of the last few months.

As the food cooked, little Ruth popped in. She was happy today but hungry as always. "Yum, that smells good," she said as she entered. She began singing and walking around Mary's hut, examining the shelves and kissing Mary on the cheek. Mary checked her bruises and was satisfied that she was healing well. Ruth felt free to sit on top of the chest and swing her legs in rhythm with her song.

John had followed Ruth into the hut, but before he could ask about the holy veil, Ruth offered, "I left the veil at home so my father can see it." Mary nodded in approval, and John did not say a word.

As Ruth continued to sing, her mother Abigail walked in. She was a woman in her mid-twenties but looked more like a woman in her forties. She was very thin, with hollow cheeks and dark circles under her black eyes. Her veil had fallen off her head and revealed disheveled black hair. Her clothes were ill-fitting and threadbare. Her skirt was too short, revealing scratches on her legs from the brambles on the hill. She was sweating from her climb and looked around nervously. She reminded John of a rabbit, twitching and ready to run at the least sign of danger.

Mary motioned to Abigail to come nearer and then touched her gently on her hand. "Please, won't you join us for lunch? Priscilla is preparing a leg of lamb with herb sauce. We have bread and fruit." Her touch had a remarkable effect on Abigail. She seemed to shake off her apprehension, and she stopped twitching. Ruth jumped off the chest and approached Abigail.

"Please, Mother, may we stay for lunch? I am very hungry, and it smells so good."

Abigail had smelled the food as she approached the hut, and her stomach was rumbling in response. "Well, I suppose there is no need to rush home. Your father will have found his jug by now and will be content for some time. We can stay a bit longer. But as soon as we eat, we must go home."

John moved the table to the center of the room and spread the mats around it. Priscilla moved the large bowl with steaming gravy to the center of the table and gave everyone a piece of bread for dipping. Then she gave everyone a small piece of mutton and passed the bowl of fruit.

Abigail began to dip her bread into the bowl and noticed that everyone else was sitting with their hands folded. She quickly drew her arm back and put her hand, still clutching the bread, in her lap. John led the prayer: "Dear Lord, thank you for this food and for bringing us our special friends today."

Mary looked at Abigail and nodded with a smile. Abigail began to warm to this woman. She had never known her and had never trusted her, but Ruth seemed to like her. The veil Ruth had brought home had intrigued her, and she wanted to know more about this family, despite the stories her mother and grandmother had told her as she was growing up. She was still on her guard and planned to leave after the meal.

Thinking of the veil at Abigail's home, John said, "Mother, as I think back to the time Jesus died, there are still some things I do not understand. I was with you much of the time, but I did not experience everything. Can you tell us the story now, so that we can share it with others?"

Abigail shot Mary a hard glance. He was talking about the man who had been crucified in disgrace in Jerusalem—the son who had been conceived outside of marriage—and the face on the veil she had looked at for hours last night. She was curious about him now. She had been a child when he died. Her parents had told her that after his death, Nazareth was an even harder place to live. Within a year of his death, her family had moved to Ephesus.

Mary nodded, put her piece of fruit down, and began.

One night, over fifteen years ago, I was eating the Passover meal. I was in a room with three other women on the second floor of a building in Jerusalem. The other two rooms were occupied by my son and his followers. We all ate unleavened bread and bitter herbs, and we shared a lamb. It was proper for the men and women to be separated, so John, you are a witness to what happened in your room.

John nodded, his mind flooding with memories of Jesus washing the men's feet, breaking the bread, and speaking of a betrayer ... many, many memories. His eyes began to water as Mary continued.

I had suspected the end of my son's life was near, but I didn't know precisely what would happen or when.

While eating in the room with the women, I saw Judas rush past our door and down the steps. I knew something was about to happen soon.

While we were cleaning up after the meal, Jesus stepped into our room and asked to speak to me alone. We went out of the room and down the narrow stairs and into the street below. The other men were already outside and gathered in a circle several paces away from us. The air was cool and getting colder. There was a steady wind blowing my robes about me. I clutched my veil tightly around my face as Jesus put his hands on my shoulders and looked into my eyes.

He whispered to me that this would be the last time we would be alone together before his death. As he drew me against his chest, he told me that this would be our last embrace. He asked me to pray for his strength and for mine. He reminded me of the story I had told him many times of Simeon's prophesy that a sword would pierce my heart. He said that prophesy would be fulfilled over the next twenty-four hours. He said that I needed to be strong for both of us. He knew how much suffering we would both bear before the next sundown.

When Jesus was a young boy, I had taught him to respond only with love when other children were selfish or cruel. Now he reminded me of that lesson. He said that I would have to forgive his tormenters. He said I would have to forgive Judas for betraying him for a bag of coins and that I would have to forgive Peter for denying him. He said that I would be tempted by Satan and that I would need many prayers to overcome that temptation.

He reminded me that what he was about to suffer was for the salvation of souls. I understood that what we had both been preparing for all of our lives was about to happen. I was shivering, and not only from the cold. He gave me one more squeeze and then turned quickly and walked down the path toward the outer wall of the city. The men followed after Jesus, and I lost sight of him quickly. I followed the group for a while; I was not willing to say good-bye so soon. But my small legs could not keep up with the quick strides of the men. Soon they were through the gate and on their way up the hill. I knew from the direction they were taking that they were heading for the garden of Gethsemane. It was one of my son's favorite places to pray.

I stood there for a while, frozen in place, with the wind whipping my clothing and almost tipping me over. I held onto the side of the gate through which they had just passed, watching their forms, now disappearing in the darkness as they ascended the hill. I knelt down and began to pray to our Father to give me strength and courage to face the next day. I prayed for my son to have the strength to follow his Father's Will. I did not want to go back to our rooms, but I knew I must. The women would be worried about me. Salome, Magdalene, and Mary were very protective of me, and I didn't want to give them cause for concern. I knew that their day tomorrow would be long and arduous.

I stood up slowly, turned around, and began to follow the path toward our rooms. Suddenly, the meal I had just eaten rebelled against my stomach and came up forcefully. I found some clean rain water that had collected in a barrel under a drain pipe and rinsed my mouth and washed my face. Then I slowly followed the narrow street back to our rented rooms.

Magdalene was waiting for me outside our building in the street. It was so dark she could not see my face, but as she held me, she could feel me trembling. She had been close to Jesus and understood much of what he had said about his destiny. As we walked back inside and neared a lantern, she took my face in her hands and could see that I had been crying. "Is this the night?" she asked.

"Yes," I said. "It starts tonight and will end tomorrow."

Magdalene said nothing more. She just nodded her head and kissed me on the forehead. Then she hooked my arm in hers and we walked upstairs to our room. She helped me to my cot and lay beside me. I told her, "There is nothing that will prevent this. It is the Father's Will for the salvation of mankind. We will help Jesus in small ways if we can. We will be with him as much as we can. But we will not stop it. The best thing we can do for him is to pray. Do you understand?" Magdalene could not speak, but she nodded yes. I continued, "Satan will be very powerful tomorrow. We must not yield to him. We must not hate those who hurt Jesus. If we hate others, we will be following Satan's will. Jesus will be brave, and we must also be brave … and forgiving. Magdalene, will you stay by me and do as the Father wishes?"

This time she found her voice and whispered, "Yes, Mother. I will stay with you. I will do as you and the Father wish. Then she held me, and we both stayed awake listening to the noises in the night. We prayed for strength to do the impossible: to watch our beloved Jesus be hurt and killed and not to hate those who would do this to him.

Mary stopped her story and looked at the faces around the table. There was a tear coming down Priscilla's face. Abigail was holding Ruth and staring at Mary in disbelief.

Abigail said, "Woman, how could you be expected to watch your son be tortured and crucified and not spit on those doing it? I would never stop hating the Romans or the members of the Sanhedrin who had him arrested. I could never forgive the man who sold him for a bag of coins. Don't the Scriptures tell us that we should take and eye for an eye and a tooth for a tooth?"

Mary turned to Abigail and answered, "My son told us to live a life of forgiveness and love. It is much harder, but the reward of his kingdom is worth the struggle."

Priscilla said, "Mother, please continue."

A few hours later, John came rushing into our room. Magdalene and I took the veils we had been using as pillows, covered our hair, and sat up. He was breathing hard and sweating, even though the evening was cool. I guessed he had run all the way back from the garden. He told us about Jesus' arrest. I told him to sit down and take some water. As he drank, I said, "There is nothing we can do at this hour, John. Let us pray for my son as he suffers through this night. At first light, we will leave for the Praetorium."

Even though it was not proper for John to be in our room, he stayed with us as we held hands and prayed. We prayed for Jesus, and we prayed for us. We prayed for the strength not to hate. John had seen his friend Judas betray Jesus with a kiss. He had seen his beloved teacher and friend bound with chains and led away as he was beaten with fists and rods.

Before daylight pierced the room, I was up slicing bread. I knew that we would need strength for the day. I forced myself to chew a bit of crust. It tasted like straw, and it took several sips of water before I could swallow it. Magdalene refused to eat or drink. John just sipped on water. I put some pieces of bread in a bag I carried under my robe. The other women were awake soon, and I told them that Jesus had been arrested and that John, Magdalene, and I were headed to the Praetorium to find him. Without a word, they stood up and prepared to leave. We were like warriors heading into battle, but our battle was not against men. Our battle would be against Satan and his demons. We knew that Satan would attempt to turn our hearts to hatred for the Jewish leaders and the Romans, but we were steadfast in our determination. We had prayed for hours and felt as if we were covered in armor.

It was still dark as we left the building and headed west toward the Antonia Fortress. As we neared the opening, we passed by one of the charcoal fires with a group of five or six people huddled around it, warming themselves. I heard a man's deep voice shout a profanity, and I turned to look. It was Peter! He continued to shout, saying, "I tell you I do not know the man!" The group suddenly fell silent, and we heard a cock crow as the sun began to rise.

Peter turned away from those around the fire and walked quickly toward our little group. When he saw me, he froze. He saw a look of sadness and disappointment in my eyes. He looked at John and saw astonishment and disbelief in his expression. Peter felt a pain so deep in his heart that he put both hands to his chest. He began to beat his breast and knelt on the ground and shouted, "Oh, Father, let me die now, for I have denied the Son of God!"

I rushed to Peter to comfort him, but he stood up quickly, turned from me, and hurried away. "Come, Mother," John said. "We must continue. We will see Peter another day."

When we arrived at the Praetorium, we were early enough to get close to the bottom of the steps that seemed to be the center of activity. We sat on the flat stone surface of the courtyard as people began to arrive. We prayed constantly. The crowd began to swell as the sun rose higher, and soon many people surrounded us. The smell became oppressive, and so many feet moving close made sitting on the ground unbearable. We stood up, waited, and prayed. Satan was already working to upset us by sending so many rude and vulgar people to stand beside us.

An hour later, the Roman guards came out into the courtyard. Some stood at the top of the steep stairway; others pushed people off of the steps and stood in a line guarding the platform. Several soldiers stood at the bottom of the steps as a barricade and faced the crowd.

Soon after, Pontius Pilate came out from a side room and stood above us. He looked tired. I don't think he had slept much that night. Then I saw Jesus being taken up from the prison below to the bottom of the steps. When Pilate motioned for him to come forward, the guards pushed Jesus roughly up the stairway. He was barely recognizable. His robe had been torn and was filthy. His face was swollen, bruised, and bleeding from his mouth and nose. His hands were tied behind his back, preventing him from wiping the fresh blood that flowed from recent blows. I could not hear what Pilate said to Jesus, but I could tell they were having a conversation, and Pilate was becoming agitated.

It seemed at one point that Pilate was going to release Jesus. He began arguing with the high priests. Pilate said that he believed Jesus was an innocent man. When I heard this, I clasped my hands to my breast, thinking perhaps there was a chance that he would be released and in my arms soon.

Then I heard Pilate bellow, "Take the man away and scourge him." Jesus was yanked back down the stairs and through a tunnel to the back of the fortress and into a courtyard surrounded by a fence about as tall as a man. Some of the crowd tried to follow Jesus through the passageway, but they were stopped by the soldiers. Then John took my arm and showed me a path around the Praetorium to the fence surrounding the courtyard where Jesus had been taken. The three women followed us. We were close enough to hear what was happening. Some people standing next to me were talking about a man that had died the week before from scourging. I cringed as I heard this.

John showed me an opening in the fence where I could see Jesus. It broke my heart to see him tied to a short column and stripped of his garments. His arms were pulled tight toward the column, and the ropes were cutting into his flesh.

John found a wooden box and moved it near me. He climbed on top of it to see what was happening. I stopped looking; it was just too hard. I could hear everything, and that was painful enough. The soldiers were laughing and telling filthy jokes. They cursed my son and each other. Some were already drunk with wine.

Then it began. I heard each lash tear my son's flesh. With each blow, I shuddered. The men continue to strike his battered body as someone counted the strokes. When the count reached twenty, they paused to rest. I could hear a trickle of water then, and I thought perhaps they were giving Jesus a cool drink. When I heard the laughter and my son moan, I knew the truth. They were urinating on His raw back. I sank to the ground. I was sitting with my hands over my face, weeping silently as they took up their whips again.

I stroked the wooden fence in an effort to let my son know I was near, but there was nothing I could do to lessen his pain. One woman near me commented that usually men being scourged would shout oaths or scream in pain. Jesus moaned but did little else. I continued to pray for some relief for my son. The guards were so cruel! They taunted him, cursed him, and I suddenly became dizzy as the world began to spin.

When I looked up, I saw a handsome young man. He was dressed in a robe that glistened with jewels and golden threads. He had long, yellow hair and an unblemished face. He looked at me with a sad expression, as if he cared for me and my son. When he spoke, my skin grew cold, and I had goose-flesh all over. My stomach turned as if I was going to vomit.

"Woman, I can help," he said in fake sympathy. "I can make his pain go away. I can give him back to you, whole and healed." Then his voice softened as if he loved me. "I can take away his pain. I can stop all of this torture and save his life. He should not have to suffer. He is a good and innocent man. All those who pretended to love him have deserted him. One *of his chosen twelve betrayed him and sold him for thirty pieces of silver. His so-called leader denied him. All of his pain is unnecessary. His death would be a senseless waste."*

He took my hand in his, and a shiver ran down my spine. I tried to take my hand back, but his hold was too strong. He continued, "All you need to do is kneel down and kiss the hem of my robe and worship me. I will give him back to you, whole and healthy."

I knew it was Satan speaking to me. I knew he was the king of all liars. He knows our weaknesses even before we do. It would have been so easy for me to kiss the hem of his golden garment. It was dangling right in front of my face. I knew he had the power to stop the torture and set my son free. I knew if I only offered my soul to his service, my son would no longer be in pain. I also knew that if I did this unspeakable thing, my son's mission would be thwarted, and Satan would hold sway over the world.

I was repulsed by him. I suddenly yanked my hand away and found my voice. "Never, never will I kneel before you. Be gone, evil one." I shouted out, "Jesus!" as loud as I could.

All of this time, John had been standing on his box, looking over the fence. When I cried out, John saw Jesus look up toward the wall. He saw Jesus' eyes spark with anger—not at the men whipping him but at the unseen evil one tempting me. Then Jesus thundered, "Be gone, Satan!" and at that, the handsome young man before me shriveled into an ugly beast with scales. He shrieked and then disappeared.

John came over to Mary and laid a hand on her shoulder. "I remember that, Mother. I remember when Jesus looked up when he heard your voice. I saw him cry out, but I didn't understand why. They continued to whip him, and I came down off my box to hold you."

"Yes, John. Jesus' prayer banished Satan from my side. It was a private temptation, and there was no need to worry you. My son and I have always been in a battle with the evil one."

John took Mary's hand and said, "Please continue, Mother."

I regained consciousness in John's arms. He was wiping my face gently, as I had been sweating through this vision. "Help me stand, John. I am all right now," I insisted. John was reluctant to let me stand. He held me tightly as he moved me toward a shade tree. I stayed there for a few minutes until I stopped shaking, and then I asked John to take me back to the fence. I wanted to be closer to my son. Mary of Magdalene had stayed near the wall with the other two women but had collapsed to the ground in grief. She was counting the lashes and sobbing. We heard one of the guards counting as well: "Thirty-seven ... thirty-eight ... thirty-nine. Done! Whew, I'm glad that is over. My arm is sore. Pass me more of that wine. I feel like I have just eaten sand."

John was overcome with anger and began cursing the guards. I put my arm on his and gave him a look that silenced him immediately.

John looked at Mary across the table. "Yes, Mother, I remember that. Your loving touch stopped my words of anger. Those men were so evil and disrespectful. I still cannot comprehend how they could be so cruel."

Mary looked upon John with a mother's love. "Yes, John, it is difficult to understand, but I tell you the truth, Satan was very active that day. Other fallen angels were all urging wicked behavior in the Jewish leaders, among the Roman soldiers, and even among Jesus' followers."

Mary looked at the faces around the table. "Be on your guard today, as well. Satan has not given up. He will test you every day. He is the cleverest deceiver of all. You may not even know when he is whispering in your ear, so be on your guard. He wants to make you as evil as those who tortured and killed my precious son."

She noticed Abigail with her arm around her daughter. Ruth was crying quietly and holding her mother's hand in one of her tiny hands. No one spoke for a long time.

Then Abigail's eyes began to water, and she wiped a tear from her face with her sleeve. She said, "Mary, I only heard rumors about your son being born to you outside of marriage. I believed he was a criminal and was punished justly. I was a young girl of only ten years when that happened. I had traveled to Jerusalem for the Passover with my parents, and I snuck outside the gates of the city to see the men hanging on the crosses. I didn't get close because the scene frightened me.

"I remember the sun disappearing at midday and the sky becoming dark. When the earth shook and people began screaming in fright, I ran back to my parents. When I returned to the room we had rented, the roof had fallen in. My father and my mother were buried under the rubble. I dug them out. They were shaken but not seriously injured. Some said that Jesus had caused the earthquake. We left Jerusalem as soon as possible.

"We lived in Nazareth only a year longer, and then we fled to Ephesus. I met and married Amos here. He is a pagan. He drinks often and beats us. I have a bitter life without hope. Can you give me hope?"

Mary spoke up with a strong voice so that all could hear. "Yes, my daughter, there is hope. It comes from my son's resurrection. He was dead on Friday, buried in a newly hewn tomb, and resurrected on Sunday morning. Forty days later, he ascended into his kingdom, where he sits at the right hand of the Father. He suffered and died to make a place for you in his kingdom. Life on this earth is not easy. Ever since the first sin by Adam and Eve, life has been hard for mankind. But remember, the time we spend on this earth is like a drop in the ocean of eternity. Our God is merciful, and because my son made the supreme sacrifice, the door to an eternity in the kingdom of heaven is open."

Abigail said through tears, "How can I ask God for forgiveness when I have been so cruel to you, dear Mother? I have not been a good mother to Ruth. How can he forgive all of that?"

Mary put her hand on Abigail's arm and said, "He loves you, my child, more than you can imagine. Just tell him now that you are sorry, and offer your life up to him. You will find peace and hope during your time on earth, and a wonderful paradise will await you after your death."

Mary then looked at the four faces around the table and said, "Bring all of your joys and sorrows, all of your hopes and despair, all that you are, and lay it down at the feet of Jesus. Surrender to him! He is your greatest friend and advocate. I am your mother, and I love all of my children with a love that surpasses all understanding. I pray for you continuously, but my children, you must understand that Jesus is the true and only source of your salvation. Only he can stand before the throne of the Father and plead for you. His blood was shed so that he could obtain that purpose and privilege."

Everyone was touched by Mary's love and message. They bowed their heads and prayed deeply and privately. Even little Ruth understood the profound words of love.

As he prayed, John felt a tugging at his heart to go to Greece with Andrew. But as he looked at Mary, he shook off the feeling. He could not bring himself to leave … not just yet.

CHAPTER NINE

A REUNION

The next afternoon, as John was repairing a broken shelf and Mary was weaving a basket, she said casually, "You know, John, I was very surprised when Jesus told me that Peter was to be the leader of his church. I was hoping he would pick you." John turned in surprise.

"Mother, why me? I was so young. Why would you think that? I was never one of the leaders."

"Well, for one thing," Mary answered, "Peter was so impetuous, and you were always so levelheaded. And you have courage. You were the only one who stayed with me throughout that terrible Friday. Everyone else fled in fear."

"Yes, Mother, I certainly cannot argue the fact that Peter leaps before thinking. I remember the time we were in the boat, fishing, not long after we had seen Jesus resurrected. Jesus was standing on the shore of the Sea of Galilee and shouted to us to cast our nets on the right side of the boat. At that point, we didn't know it was Jesus calling out to us. We did it anyway, as we were not having any success catching anything before then, and we were all pretty hungry.

"When we pulled in all of the fish, I realized who had called out to us, and I told Peter, 'It is the Lord.' He got so excited he jumped into the water and swam to shore. He reminded me of a small child who sees his father coming home and drops everything, even a favorite plaything, and leaps into his father's arms. He forgot all about the fish, the boat, and all of us. We were left to row that heavy boat to shore without his help.

"We had a good laugh with him as he dried his clothes over the fire while we ate the fish and bread Jesus had prepared. Jesus laughed with us. We still tease Peter about his rush to do things without thinking."

"That's exactly why I was surprised that my son picked Peter," Mary continued. "Even though he was one of the older apostles, he sometimes acted like a child. I asked Jesus one time why he picked Peter, and he said that he knew Peter's true heart. He knew Peter was strong-willed and that his tenacity would hold the small band of followers together after his departure from this earth. Jesus knew that once Peter made his mind up to do something, he would put all of his heart and soul into it. Jesus knew that no one could discourage Peter from his mission. He also knew that Peter had a great love for God. He knew that Peter had great faith, even though he also knew that Peter would deny him three times. Jesus knew that Peter would grow in courage and faith over time. Jesus loved you very much, John, but he had another job for you: taking care of me!" Mary giggled like a small girl as she said this.

"Well, I'm not sure I have done a good job of that lately, leaving you alone for four days. I still feel terrible about that. Will you forgive me?"

Mary put down her basket and went over to John and put her arm on his shoulder. "My dear son, do not think of that any longer. You were doing what God wanted of you. There are many more important tasks now than taking care of me. The sands are shifting these days."

After a pause, she added, "My son, put down your work and sit with me. I have something very important to tell you." John put his tools on the floor and helped Mary back to her seat on the mat. He sat close beside her.

She took John's hands in both of her hands. "I have kept a secret for many years, but I feel it is time to share it with you. I will be leaving you soon. The Holy Spirit is whispering this to me. My job here on this earth is finished. I am tired, and I want to go home. Let me tell you a story."

On the Sunday morning of my son's resurrection, long before the sun came up, Jesus came to me privately in our room. I had been lying next to Mary of Magdalene that evening. The room took on a warm glow, and I opened my eyes. I saw my son. His face was healed, and the wounds from the crown of thorns were gone. He looked beautiful. He came near me and took my hand. He guided me out of the room and into a small hallway where we found a narrow bench. The house was very still, as everyone was sleeping deeply.

Jesus told me that I would remain on this earth for many more years as a favor to the Father. It was all part of His plan for the salvation of mankind. I had many tasks to perform for the survival of the fledgling church. It was necessary for me to be a mother to many, so that my son's life and death would not be in vain. It was necessary for me to be the North Star, the guiding light for the followers left to continue my son's work.

He told me that I would be taken into heaven when the Father judged that my life on earth was complete. He told me that when the time came, no one would find my corpse, and that I would go into heaven, body and soul together.

Mary looked directly into John's eyes. "One day, John, you will simply find me missing. On that day, look for flowers on your mat. That is the sign and the final gift I will leave for you. When you see fresh flowers on your mat, you will know that I have gone to my son's kingdom and that I am resting in his arms."

Throughout this discourse, John sat motionless, rapt in the mystery Mary was revealing to him.

"Dear John, when I leave here to be with my son, I will also be able to be with you whenever you need me. I don't know how this will happen, but I *do* know I will not desert you. I love you more than you can imagine, and I will never be far from your side."

Mary gave John's hands a little squeeze as she continued.

"You can talk to me, and I'm sure I will be able to help you and any others who ask me. Our family is scattering among many foreign lands, and it is time for you to go also. You should not be stuck in this hut taking care of an old woman. The best thing I can do for you now is to go to my son's kingdom."

John was stunned and didn't know what to say. Mary released her hold on his hand, rolled up her basket-weaving, and lay down on her mat as John stood up. She pulled her blanket over her head and faced the wall to hide her tears. John leaned over and gave her a long embrace. Tears welled up in his eyes and slid down his tanned face. He loved this mother so much.

John had lost his own mother a year before he met Jesus, and this blessed woman had been given to him as his mother while Jesus was dying on the cross. What a gift!

John thought back to the first time he had seen Mary in Cana. He had felt drawn to her immediately, and he always wanted to be close to her and protect her.

Perhaps, John thought, his love for Mary may have been why Jesus favored him so much, why Jesus called him *Beloved*. John was young, yes, and sometimes needed more guidance than the others, but he also was very close to Jesus' mother and loved her tenderly. That's why, as frightened as he was, John could never leave her alone during Jesus' agony. John had stayed with Mary and held her, doing what he could to console her, even when his own heart was hammering with fear and tearing apart with grief. They had a special bond, and life without Mary would be very empty.

As Mary faced the wall in silent prayer, John got on his knees and began to pray. He prayed for guidance from the Holy Spirit. He prayed for courage to do the Father's Will. He prayed for consolation to ease his loneliness when the time came for Mary to leave. He prayed for faith in her promise, that even though she would depart from this earth, he would not be left without her guidance and love.

Mary rested for about an hour and then got up to prepare their evening meal. John had already started cleaning vegetables. As they worked quietly side by side, they heard the sound of many voices and footsteps on the path leading up to the stone hut. This was a remote spot, far from the main streets of the town, and it was an alarming sound. John stood up immediately and went outside the doorway. To his amazement, Peter stood there in apparently good health, together with Mark, Aquila, and Priscilla.

John was speechless as he embraced Peter. Then he stood back and found his voice, "How did you arrive so quickly? How is your health? How are your wounds from the lashings?"

John began to take Peter's cape from his shoulders to examine his back.

Peter, never one to allow others to fuss over him, pulled his cape back on and pushed John back with surprising strength. "I'm fine, I'm fine! Don't bother with me," Peter said gruffly. Then he ducked his head to enter the hut and rushed toward Mary. She was standing beside her mat, craning her neck to see who was approaching. The hut was dark and the lamplight was dim. Peter drew her close and embraced her.

"Dear Mother, it is so good to find you well. Something urged me to travel quickly and come to you as soon as possible. My wounds healed shortly after Mark arranged for my release. I ate well, rested well, and in one day I was ready to travel. I needed to see you, to hold your hand, to look into your lovely blue eyes once more. I missed you so much! The journey here was an easy one. We were able to catch a ship the first day we looked for passage. The sea was calm, and the wind was in our sails. I was healthy enough to walk from the shore across the mountain to this holy place."

Peter was a large man, and Mary nearly disappeared in his embrace. He smelled of the sea and dust of the road. He did not reek of prison and sickness. Mary was familiar with the smell of a man newly released from prison: a musty odor of death. She was glad Peter had taken the opportunity to bathe and wash his clothes before greeting her. She guessed Priscilla had seen to that.

Mary gently broke from his embrace and led him to a seat on a mat closer to the lamp. The light was better here and she wanted to get a good look at him. His beard had once been black but was now almost completely grey. His hair was curly and course. It was as thick and unruly as it had always been, but now there was a shiny, bald spot on the top of his head that reflected the lamplight. Mary touched it tenderly. Peter took her hand, kissed it, and helped her to her stool. He was thinner than she remembered, and the lines in his face, especially around his eyes, had deepened. Peter spoke aloud her thoughts. "We are all aging, perhaps a bit faster than we like. But you look wonderful! You still have the face of a young girl. You still have those beautiful eyes … so full of love."

"Ah," Mary replied, "but I do not have the strength I used to have."

The rest of the company had been waiting outside, wanting to give Mary and Peter some privacy. Priscilla had been busy around the fire pit, directing others to gather more wood and build a nice fire for dinner. Since the hut was small, Priscilla planned to serve the meal outside. She directed Mark and Aquila to carry the table out, so they could use it for the food as it was prepared.

She had brought some loaves of fresh bread, and Mark had brought some fresh fish to fry. Aquila had carried a basket of fruit and vegetables. When all was ready, Priscilla came into the hut and took Mary's hand to guide her to the large flat rock near the fire outside.

Mark brought news of Mary's family from Nazareth. He told her that Mary Salome, the wife of Cleophas and mother of four apostles, had just died. She had been with Mary through her son's suffering and death and had remained with her as they washed Jesus' body and put him in the tomb. Mark said that when Mary Salome died, Simon and Jude were away preaching the gospel and did not know of their mother's death. James "the less" and Joseph had remained with their mother as she grew close to death. After her burial, they also left to preach the news of Jesus.

Mary took Mark's hand and said a short prayer with him for her cousin Mary Salome and her sons. She knew the times were dangerous for those left in Galilee and for those traveling to strange lands.

After the prayer, she turned from Mark, wiped a tear with her sleeve, and prayed silently, *Dear Lord, when is it my turn to be with you in your kingdom?*

As those outside were finding seats around the fire and waiting for the fish to cook, there was a sound of voices below on the path. More travelers were approaching, but because of the fading sun, their shapes were indistinguishable.

Then a booming voice proclaimed, "I hope you saved some fish for me!"

Paul had returned with Timothy, Luke, Barnabas, Erastus, Tychicus, and Gaius. Everyone stood up to welcome their friends. These men had not come empty-handed. Barnabas carried a small lamb up the hill on his shoulders and Gaius was carrying two jugs of wine.

It was the first time in fifteen years that so many had been together. Some of their "family" was still far away, dead, or in jail; but this was quite a reunion nonetheless. It was a lot of excitement for Mary.

Luke and Barnabas stood back until everyone had greeted Paul. Peter was the last to embrace Paul, and guided him to the seat next to him. Even though these men had been known to quarrel vigorously, they still loved one another as much as brothers. They shared such a strong love and passion for the Lord that they were bound together.

John exchanged a knowing look with Mary and then turned and went into the hut and walked directly over to Mary's chest. He pulled out a heavy bundle from the bottom and took it outside to the table. He gently unrolled the length of cloth, and out tumbled the large chalice that Jesus had used during their last supper that fateful Thursday. John brought the chalice to Peter, and he took it reverently as John sat beside Mary.

Many were still standing around the fire exchanging embraces and greetings. Barnabas and Timothy were busy putting the lamb on a spit over the fire. Luke brought the jugs of wine over to Peter.

Mary motioned to Luke to sit beside her so that John was on her right hand and Luke on her left. Peter said, "My brothers and sisters, please be seated." Peter poured some of the wine into the chalice John had brought to him. Those who did not recognize the chalice were told immediately in whispers that it had been held by Jesus the night he was arrested.

As the silence flowed over the group like a warm breeze, Mary noticed a small, shadowy figure at the crest of the hill. As the form came into focus, Mary motioned for Ruth to sit beside her. The little girl squeezed in between Mary and Luke. As Mary kissed Ruth on the forehead, she noticed two more shadows coming up over the rise. As they approached the firelight, Abigail and Amos came hesitantly toward the group. Amos had brought a big basket of rice cakes and vegetables to add to the feast. Mary motioned for others to move closer together to make room for the new guests to be seated. After kissing Mary on the cheek Ruth moved to sit next to her mother.

Tears of joy began streaming down Mary's face. She lifted her arms toward the sky and tilted her head back toward the stars. Everyone suddenly became silent and looked toward Mary as she began her prayer.

"Our Father, who art in heaven, Hallowed be Thy name."

Then Ruth joined in the prayer as Mary had taught her: "Thy kingdom come."

Paul and Peter's voices were heard next. "Thy Will be done."

All of the company spontaneously joined hands and continued, "On this earth as it is in heaven. Give us this day our daily bread, and forgive us our trespasses as we forgive those who trespass against us."

Abigail and Amos looked at each other and then at the beautiful woman who had forgiven them. They realized that they were being asked to forgive one another as well.

The prayer continued, "Lead us not into temptation, but deliver us from evil."

Everyone paused and reflected on how many times they had been led down the path of temptation, on how clever Satan could be and how strong they needed to be. It was a daily struggle to put on the armor against Satan. Their voices swelled to heaven, "For thine is the kingdom, the power, and the glory, now and forever. Amen!"

After the prayer, Mary nodded to Peter, and he said, "Lord, we do this in remembrance of you." Peter lifted a loaf of bread, blessed it, broke it in two, and passed the halves—one to his right and one to his left. Then he repeated the words Jesus had said the night before he died. Each person receiving the bread broke off a piece, put the morsel into his mouth with a silent prayer, and passed the bread to the next person. After the loaf was consumed, Peter lifted the large chalice of wine, blessed it, and passed it around. There wasn't a sound as people took a sip of the wine and passed it on. After the chalice returned to Peter, everyone sat motionless, heads down in reverent prayer. Many felt God's presence and shed tears of joy. It was a feeling of peace and overwhelming love.

John looked around the circle and thought that everyone here had been called by God to this place at this time. He believed that they all had special missions to carry out from this time until the ends of their lives. Everyone was different: some large, some small, some new to the faith, and some with great faith and knowledge in God's word. It was a beautiful mixture of people and truly representative of the body of Christ.

He spoke up and said, "This little spot on earth is about as close to heaven as a place on earth can get." Everyone nodded and wished that this feeling of love and peace would last forever. Soon, maybe tomorrow, someone would be arrested, someone might suffer from blows or hunger or bad weather … but just now, this little band of followers was together, and peace permeated the hillside.

Finally, little Ruth broke the silence. "Mother, when you said, 'Lead us not into temptation, but deliver us from evil,' what did you mean?"

Mary smiled lovingly. "Well, let me tell you about temptations from the evil one. I was tempted frequently. Satan, the leader of the angels who turned from God, has been tempting me all of my life, even when I was your age. He wanted me to disobey my parents; he wanted me to be selfish; and he wanted me to lie. But when I felt these urges, I would fall on my knees and pray to the almighty One to banish him, and he would leave me in peace for a while. Satan was especially angry when my son was living inside of me. He tried to have me and my son killed." Mary put both of her hands protectively over her womb where the Savior had once lived.

She continued, "Many people in Nazareth wanted to stone me, and so my family helped me to hide until Joseph could take me to my cousin Elizabeth's home. He didn't bring me back to Nazareth until he felt it was safe for me."

Abigail looked down at her hands in shame. She knew that her parents and grandparents were among the group who had talked about dragging Mary beyond the wall of the city to stone her.

Mary went on. "When our heavenly Father sent protection for my life, Satan tried to take my soul through daily temptations. He would whisper in my ear how hard my life was since I chose to carry the baby before my marriage to Joseph. He told me I was a disgrace and an embarrassment to my mother and father. He told me I was making all of their lives harder and that I should just walk out into the wilderness to die.

"Later, when Jesus was born, he told me to leave Joseph and baby Jesus and go back to my mother. He told me I was too young and inexperienced to be the mother of the Savior and that Jesus would be better off with another mother.

"He tempted me each day with riches and false promises. When we were hungry, he tempted me with delicacies. When we were cold, he tempted me with warm blankets. Usually I could brush him away by holding my son or just calling out his holy name."

"Like you did when Jesus was being scourged?" Abigail asked.

"Yes, exactly," Mary responded, and then continued. "When Jesus was older, I would call him to me, and Satan would flee. You see, Satan is a coward at heart. He knows my son can defeat him. And he did defeat Satan with his death and resurrection.

Satan was, and still is, my most constant enemy. I draw strength from my spouse, the Holy Spirit, Father God, and my son and Savior."

Everyone around the circle remained silent throughout this discourse. No one had ever heard Mary talk of these things. In the silence, Ruth stood up, opened her package, and brought the veil over to Mary. "Dear Mother, here is the veil you let me borrow." Mary held it up for all to see, as Ruth went over to sit in her mother's lap. As the image of Jesus' face was illuminated by the firelight, many gasped. Only Luke, Peter, and John had seen the veil before this time. Some had heard rumors that the veil existed, and some had never known about it. They all watched as Mary carefully folded the veil, kissed it, and put it inside the large pocket of her gown.

After a long pause, Amos stood up and said, "In front of all of these witnesses and God, I want to confess my sins and profess my desire to be baptized. I have been gazing upon this face that you just saw for many hours. Somehow, I know ..." Amos paused to compose himself as he wiped away a tear. "Even more than knowing, I *feel* how much this man suffered for my sins. I ask for his forgiveness."

Amos took Abigail by one hand and Ruth by the other and urged them to stand. Then he looked into their eyes and said, "I ask your forgiveness also." Looking at Mary, he continued. "I have been touched by the Spirit of God, and I want to serve Him. I never want to disappoint Him again. I want to be at peace with my wife, my daughter, and my God.

Abigail and Ruth both said, "I want to be baptized too!" John was already on his feet, tears streaming down his cheeks. He picked up the gourd, filled it with water, and handed it to Peter. Peter asked Paul to stand with him as they baptized the family in front of the group around the fire.

Amos, Abigail, and Ruth all fell to their knees as Peter and Paul approached them. Peter poured the water over Amos' head and said in unison with Paul, "We baptize you in the name of the Father, the Son, and the Holy Spirit." They repeated this ritual with Abigail and little Ruth as everyone remained silent, overwhelmed with God's love.

When they had taken their seats, Mary stood up and said through her tears, "When you come together as brothers and sisters to pray with me, I cry tears of joy. I tell you the truth, my little ones: it is my heart's desire that you feel my love for you. Come to me and let me hold you close to my heart while I may, for I shall not be with you much longer. Lucifer and his fallen angels are strong at work. They will not desist. You must continue to come to the aid of your mother." At this, Mary paused and spread her arms out to the people.

She said with a steady voice, "You must continue to be strong. I know your sorrows and frustrations. Please remember every day how very much the Father, my son, and the Holy Spirit love you! Be kind and gentle to each other. Love each other as the Father loves you. Support each other. Most importantly, pray together. Pray from the heart, my little ones. Your life should be prayer, and prayer should be your life. You cannot fully understand the power of prayer. Continue to pray for conversions, peace, and the Father's mercy upon the world. Pray, pray, pray! My love and blessings are with you always, my dear ones. Come to my precious son, your sweet brother, and allow him to remove your burdens and sorrows. Allow the Holy Spirit into your hearts. Finally, go in love and peace. You are children of the Light. You are loved and treasured. Praise Jesus now and always."

Mary looked at the spit over the fire and said, "I think the lamb and fish are ready to eat. Let us have our banquet! This is all so wonderful. Let us be joyful tonight. We are all together for the first time in a long, long while. My son's message is spreading across the world, and more and more people are consecrating their hearts and lives to his sacred heart. I feel the presence of the Father, the Holy Spirit, and my son here with us on this hillside. As Peter broke the bread tonight and repeated my son's words, 'Take and eat; this is my body. Take and drink; this is my blood,' God came here to this small spot in the universe to be with us. He is still here. So let us be joyful and eat!"

Barnabas scrambled over to the lamb with his knife and began cutting off pieces as Erastus held a platter. Priscilla passed baskets of vegetables and bread. Luke put the hot pieces of fish on another platter and carried it around the circle. The wine jugs and water jug were passed from person to person as they took sips or filled goblets. People were laughing and singing and talking. The stars above were bright, and the moon was full. The air was filled with the aroma of the cooked meat and fish, mixed with a beautiful scent of wildflowers.

As people began to eat, the group became quiet once again. Mary, too excited to eat, looked from face to smiling face and with a strong voice said, "Jesus always made me smile when he was near. He was such a good little boy. He loved to laugh. Do you remember?" She directed this question to the three men present who had known Jesus. John, Peter, and Mark nodded.

Mary said, "Let me tell you all a little story." As people continued to eat, they leaned in closer to hear.

When Jesus was very small and just learning to walk, he loved to toddle after Joseph as he worked. Joseph would stop from time to time and pick up Jesus and play their favorite game. Joseph would toss Jesus into the air and catch him. It worried me a bit. I was afraid Joseph would drop Jesus, but Jesus would laugh so much, I didn't have the heart to ask Joseph to stop.

Sometimes, when they knew I was watching, they would play their game just to tease me. Then all three of us would laugh until our sides hurt. Even as a small boy, Jesus had a hearty laugh.

Sometimes Jesus would lift his arms for me to pick him up, and I would spin him around and around. We would say "wheeee" as we laughed and spun in circles. His laughter was such a delight, we would both collapse on the floor, hugging and kissing."

"I was still a young girl, so I enjoyed these games as much as my son. I'm afraid my old bones would not be able to do much spinning today."

Mary grabbed her hip in demonstration as she began to rise to fill cups with water. Priscilla put a gentle hand on her shoulder and offered, "Let me do that, Mother."

Mary kissed Priscilla's hand and sat back down as she said, "Bless you, child." She looked around the circle and continued.

As time went on, Jesus and Joseph had little secret projects and would surprise me with a treasure they had made for me. Jesus would laugh as I showed my excitement and wonder.

"Look," Mary said as she reached into the deep pocket of her gown. "I still have one of their gifts!" She held a small wooden carving of a dove in the palm of her hand. Mary passed it around the circle as everyone remarked how beautiful it was. The feather details were almost worn off with gentle handling. It was obvious that this had been a treasure for years.

Mary turned to her little friend and said, "Ruth, dear, you keep it. I'm sure Jesus would want you to have it. He loved children so much. "

Everyone who had known Jesus nodded in agreement. Ruth held it close to her face and let the firelight reveal the dove's details. Abigail said to Mary, "It will be a treasure in our home always. Thank you." With that, Abigail stood up and kissed Mary on the cheek. Then she returned to her seat, giving Ruth a loving squeeze.

Mary pointed to the wooden sculpture and said, "Ruth, keep the dove near you always, and any time you are frightened or afraid, let it remind you to pray to the Holy Spirit for peace."

Mary turned to the others around the circle and asked, "What is your favorite memory of Jesus?"

John laughed loudly and spoke up. "I remember the day he walked into the house of a synagogue official. We could hear people weeping and wailing about his dead little girl. When Jesus walked into the room where the girl was laid out on her cot, he took the child by the hand and told her to sit up. Amazingly, she sat up and then embraced Jesus. He helped her out of bed and held her elbow as she walked into her mother's open arms. Her father began crying with joy and awe.

"Everyone was speechless, except for Jesus and the little girl. After hugging her parents, she went back to Jesus. We watched as they were animated with private conversation. They began laughing out loud over something Jesus had said to her. It seemed as if they had known each other for years; they were so familiar and relaxed with each other's company. Then Jesus turned to the little girl's mother and told her to feed the child. He gave the little girl one more hug, and then we all left the house."

Mark said, "I remember that Jesus used to tease Peter about the time he walked on water ... for a few steps. Jesus liked to describe Peter's face as he first stepped out of the boat, and then—" Mark paused as he looked at Peter. "And then, as he began sinking. Peter would laugh, just as he is laughing now, when he remembered the story. Jesus said Peter was like a child who takes his first steps toward his parent and then realizes he is not so steady and falls. Jesus and Peter would laugh and slap each other on the back until tears streamed down their cheeks, remembering that day. Peter has grown so much in faith since then that, if it happened today, he could walk all the way across the Sea of Galilee without sinking!"

Everyone around the fire laughed at this, and those near Peter slapped him on the back in friendship and affirmation. Peter laughed too, remembering how impetuous he was. He stood up and walked around the fire to Mark and gave him a firm slap on the back and boomed, "Yes, little brother, I always leap before looking. Sometimes my faith makes me act like a child ... but did our Lord not say that we must be like a little child before we may enter into the Father's kingdom?" He winked at Mother Mary, and she nodded affirmatively.

Peter said, "I remember the time that people were bringing children to Jesus. It was a day when I knew our Lord was very tired, and I told the children and their parents to go away. The children were so noisy and dirty! They obeyed me and headed down the path with their backs bowed in sadness. Jesus called me to him and said that I should run after the children and call them back. They hadn't gotten far, and when I beckoned them, they turned and began running toward Jesus. He had been sitting on a flat rock, and when the children came crashing into his open arms, they almost knocked him off!

"Jesus laughed so hard. He loved it. Some of the children were clinging to his arms, and two little girls were behind him braiding his hair. Jesus made silly faces and laughed with them. His laughter was infectious. All of the people around, including me, were laughing as free as children. Then suddenly, Jesus' mood changed, and he told the children to stand in front of him. Jesus placed his hands on each little head, one by one, and blessed them. The children sensed peace in his presence and freedom from fear."

There was a long pause as people imagined the scene. Mary broke the silence. "One of my favorite memories of my son was when Jesus visited me in the early morning hours of his resurrection." She looked around the circle at surprised expressions as people stopped chewing. No one, except John, knew that Mary was the first to see the resurrected Savior.

She continued, "One of the things he said to me is that when I come home to his kingdom, I will have many children to enjoy. I only had one baby here on earth, but in my next life, God will give me all of the babies that die before they are born. I will scoop them up into my lap and surround them with my arms. We will laugh, play games, and sing songs."

Silence fell upon the group once again as they marveled at the special woman in their midst.

Then, Mary stood up, extended her arms, and said, "My children, I give you my motherly love and blessing. It is my heart's desire to lead all of my children toward greater holiness. Live your faith! Let your light shine for all the world to see. If you deny my son before your fellow man, he will deny you before the Father. Hunger for those things which feed the spirit. Shun the evil that this world has to offer. Satan is very cunning and he will lead you astray if he can. Prayer is your greatest defense. Pray for the Holy Spirit to come into your hearts. Pray for the love and peace that my son so willingly offers. Surrender your will to my son, and walk in grace. Tell all who will listen. Thank you for your willingness to do as God asks. Good-night, and may the peace of God be with you. Praise be to Jesus!"

After speaking these words, Mary turned slowly and walked into her hut. She took the veil with Jesus' image out of her pocket and placed it carefully back into the chest. She took off her sandals and knelt in prayer beside her mat for several minutes. After praising God, she took off her outer robe and veil. She sat down, rolled her veil to use as a pillow, and placed it under her head. She covered herself with a blanket and fell into a peaceful sleep.

The group outside began cleaning up the remnants of food. Paul and Peter sat and talked long into the night about the next places they would visit. John and Luke talked about their great love for Mary and how they could care for her during the next few months. The women put the food into baskets and left them just inside the hut, being careful not to wake Mary. Amos picked up Ruth and took Abigail's hand as they headed down the hill to their home.

Priscilla and Aquila, seeing there was nothing more to do, walked arm in arm down the path to their home in Ephesus. John went into the hut to sleep just inside the door.

The others found places on the roof and around the fading fire. It was a clear, warm night, and the sky was bright with a full moon and countless stars. Most people were still thinking about the words Mary had said as she departed the group. They were thinking about the tasks before them and what God wanted each to do. Each man knew that he had been selected for a particular reason and mission. They all fell into a deep sleep without fear or anxiety. It was, indeed, a bit of heaven on earth.

CHAPTER TEN

FLOWERS ON A MAT

The next morning, as Mary drifted from sleep into consciousness, she sensed something different in the air. She always felt the presence of the Holy Spirit, but this morning, there was a special feeling of lightness and love. It was as if he was closer than he had been in a long time. It reminded her of the feeling she had experienced when the Holy Spirit filled her with his love and Jesus began growing in her womb. It was something she could never explain, even to her mother or Joseph. It was a feeling of great love and peace. It was so overpowering that it brought tears of joy to her eyes.

As she lay on her mat watching the first rays of sunlight peeking through the bottom of the door, she wondered why she should feel so good. She said a prayer of thanksgiving for another day in which to serve God.

The sounds outside the hut drew her focus as the men began moving about. Mary rolled over to face the room and saw that she was alone in the hut. John's mat was rolled up and placed in the corner where he usually stowed it. The large water jug that was always placed beside the door was gone. "John has already headed down the hill to get water," she said to herself softly. "I should get up and see if any of the men would like something to eat."

Mary sat up slowly, and the overpowering feeling of the Holy Spirit's presence did not leave her. She braided her hair, put on her veil, and stood up. She reached for her outer robe hanging from a peg on the wall. After adjusting her garments, she noticed that the feeling did not leave.

The usual aches and pains Mary experienced after rising were not with her this morning. Her fingers were not stiff or sore. She stretched them out and made a fist several times to test the new flexibility she now had. Her wounded knee did not ache as she moved. She sensed that something wonderful was about to happen.

Mary sat on the stool and thought about that day, fifteen years ago, when she had seen her precious son newly risen from the tomb.

That Sunday morning, three days after his death, Mary Magdalene rushed into the upper room to announce that she had seen the Savior. Mother Mary was not surprised, for she had also seen her risen son three hours earlier.

As Mary lay sleeping, Jesus had come into her room and touched her cheek gently. He spoke one word: "Mother." She opened her eyes and, in the dim light of the oil lamp, could see his handsome face. The face that had been so cruelly beaten, that had been swollen and bruised, was now unblemished and beautiful. Jesus put his hand gently under her head and helped her to sit up. They embraced quietly, and when they moved apart, Mary put her hands on the sides of her son's now-perfect face and kissed him as she had done thousands of times before—once on each cheek and once on the forehead.

Jesus held her hand in his precious, wounded hands. Mary could see the jagged holes left by the nails. She rubbed one hole with her thumb instinctively, raised his hand to her lips, and kissed it. A tear slipped out of her eye and down her cheek.

So as not to disturb the others sleeping nearby, they moved to the hallway and spoke in whispers.

Jesus told her that he would ascend into heaven in forty days. Mary asked if he would take her with him. He shook his head sadly. "There is more the Father needs you to do on this earth." She bowed her head with this knowledge but accepted it bravely as she had accepted God's Will all of her life.

Jesus put one hand on Mary's cheek and continued, "It is your job to reassure the apostles and other followers that I will never leave them. Help them develop the courage to face persecutions for my sake. Reinforce what I have been teaching the last three years. When they become confused or frustrated, guide them back to God's Will, for you know it perfectly."

Jesus admired his mother so much. She was strong—stronger than any of the men when it came to understanding and following God's Will. Jesus knew that his mother had been chosen by the Father even before her birth. She had been given special graces and filled with the Holy Spirit all her life. Jesus told his blessed mother, "You must continue to be strong, so the apostles will have a guiding light when times get tough."

Jesus took his hand from her cheek, raised Mary's hand to his lips, kissed it, and said, "You need to be their comfort and counselor after I am gone. Once the Holy Spirit enlightens them, your yoke will be lighter, but until then, you must be here to show them how to be brave. Even after the Holy Spirit fills them with his gifts, they will continue to have weak moments. Satan will never be far from them, tempting them constantly. He will be trying to undo all that I have done. You need to stand firm until their faith is strong enough to carry on without you."

Mary stared into Jesus' soft brown eyes as he continued. "Tell your stories of our lives to all who will listen. Encourage those you trust to write down these stories for all of my followers in times to come. One day, when the Father determines that your job on earth is done and the apostles no longer need your help, Gabriel will visit you. This special messenger will take you to heaven to join me, our Father, and the Holy Spirit for all of eternity. It will be a wonderful day, and all of the souls in heaven will celebrate your homecoming."

Jesus knew that the apostles would need a sign that Mary was unharmed when this happened. He did not want John to think that she had been arrested or taken away by evil men. Jesus told her, "On the day that Gabriel comes for you, lay flowers on John's mat as a sign that you are not hurt but taken into heaven." With these words, Jesus kissed her on the cheek and quietly left.

As Mary sat gazing out the door of her hut, she thought that perhaps this was the special day she had long awaited. She imagined what it would be like to be in her son's arms once again. She closed her eyes and sighed from the joy this image brought to her mind.

"If this is the day," Mary thought, "I must be prepared." She stood up and went outside into the early morning mist to collect some flowers from the hillside.

She found the men milling about, rolling up their bedding and putting wood on the fire to heat some of the food left from their feast the night before. As each man looked up and saw Mary coming from the hut, he came to her, bowed, and asked for her blessing. Mary laid her hands on each head and said a prayer to God to bless and keep him on the path of righteousness.

After blessing each man, Mary turned and walked up the hill where she knew some wildflowers were blooming. When she reached the patch of blossoms, she was amazed that she had not been hampered by her knee during the climb.

"I came up as easily as a child," she thought. She felt like dancing and singing in the morning sunlight, but she checked herself, as the men were not far off. Mary picked several of the small, white, star-shaped flowers and quickly walked back down the hill and into her hut.

She took a small beaker from the shelf and arranged the flowers in it. "I will put water into it as soon as John gets back with the jug," she thought. Mary placed the beaker on the table and admired their beauty. "Just in case," she said quietly.

Restlessly, she looked around for something else to do. Mary peeked outside once again. The men were busy talking and eating. As she listened, she heard them discussing plans for travel and what groups of people they hoped to convert next. She smiled at their eagerness to convert others for her son.

She turned back inside the hut, unable to stand still.

Then she saw him. Gabriel stood there in the back of the room, smiling, radiating light and warmth. He bowed before her and said, "Hail, Mary, full of grace."

Mary gasped in excitement. She felt like a child again. Gabriel nodded at the flowers on the table. "I see you are ready to go," he said with a mischievous smile.

Mary giggled like a girl and nodded. She turned and walked over to the corner and unrolled John's mat. She almost danced over to the table. She took the flowers from the beaker and put them lovingly in the place where John rested his head. She reflected for a moment how much she would miss him and the others, but then she glanced back at Gabriel and quickly walked toward the magnificent angel.

Gabriel thought she moved like a young girl, and he smiled broadly, watching her. She reminded him so much of the first time he had seen her in her room years ago, although she was not frightened this time.

Then Gabriel asked Mary a question he had pondered for a long time. "Blessed Mother, knowing what you know now—all of the pain, the ridicule, the flight into Egypt, the hunger and thirst, watching your son suffer and die, the difficult years without him—" He paused and looked deeply into her cornflower-blue eyes. "Would you make the same decision and give me the same answer as you did the first day we met?"

Mary looked up into his beautiful eyes and said without hesitation, "Absolutely."

Gabriel's smile deepened as he stretched out his hand. Mary took his large, strong hand as many other angels appeared suddenly, singing and bowing before her. Mary recognized those voices. It was the same wondrous sound she had heard on the night her son was born, but it was a different song. Before, they sang of her son and peace on earth; now it was a song honoring her.

The angels began to bow before her as they sang. Some moved closer and touched her arms and shoulders. Some sat on the floor at her feet and gently touched the hem of her gown. Gabriel, keeping her hand in his, nodded, and the entire assemblage began a slow ascent.

Mary blinked, and suddenly she was above the hut. She looked down as the hut became smaller and smaller in the landscape. She saw the town of Ephesus, the mountains, and even the sea become smaller and smaller.

Mary wondered briefly what the men below were seeing and hearing. Could they hear the angels singing?

Soon the earthly shapes became unrecognizable, as Mary and the angels rose higher and higher. Her gaze shifted to the heavenly beings around her and then to the sky above. It was now black and dotted with stars—more stars than she had ever seen before. Her heart was filled with so much love, it was about to burst. It was pounding so hard, she thought surely the angels could hear it over their singing.

Mary closed her eyes for a second, and when she opened them she was standing by a beautiful gate. The pillars of the gate were made of amethyst, and the doors of the gate were glimmering like pearls. Two imposing angels with flaming swords stood outside the gate. They bowed before her. As Mary walked forward, the doors opened, and a bright light made her blink.

Then she saw her precious son. He was radiant in a pure white gown. He raced toward her and embraced her with joy and tenderness. Her arms wrapped around his back, and they held one another for a long, long time. Mary felt their hearts beating with the same rhythm.

When they broke apart, the angels made a collective gasp. Mary had been transformed from an old woman to the most beautiful young woman they had ever seen. Mary looked down and saw that her old, worn gown had been replaced by a shining white robe with a golden sash. On her feet were golden sandals. The angels broke out in a new chorus of alleluias. Their queen, their mother, was finally home.

Jesus took his beloved mother by the hand and led her down the street before them, pointing to the beauty all around.

Others began to join them on their walk. Joseph, her earthly companion for thirty years, came forward. He was healthy, young, and handsome. They embraced and continue to walk on. Mary met her mother, her father, and her cousin Salome. They looked so young and beautiful. She had never seen her mother like this, but there was no doubt it was she. She soon found Elizabeth and John and Zachariah. There was old Simeon—although now, he was young and vibrant with beautiful clear eyes. He ran up to Mary and reminded her how he had held her infant son and pronounced him to be the Savior. Mary was overwhelmed as others she had known during her life on earth came to welcome her home.

Somehow she knew who they all were, even though they looked so young and perfect. Everyone had a glow about them. Jesus, knowing her thoughts, whispered, "The glow is from God's holy grace and love."

As they continued to walk, Jesus pointed out the trees, flowers, animals, gurgling brooks, and the birds of the air. Some of the animals began to join their parade. Mary had never seen such animals on earth. One resembled a large yellow cat with black spots. It purred as it rubbed its head against Mary's leg. She giggled with delight and reached down to pet it.

Jesus squeezed her hand and said, "Now it is time to meet our Father. He has something very special waiting for you."

A NEW BEGINNING

John walked back up the hill carrying the large jug full of fresh water. He was thinking of the evening before. It had been so special. He said a brief prayer of thanks for the wonderful reunion they had all experienced and the blessings he had received.

As he crested the hill and came in site of Mary's hut, he thought he saw a lightning bolt above the hut. He blinked for a moment to clear his vision. The sky was bright blue with only wispy clouds in sight. Then he thought he heard singing, but it was only for an instant.

As he reached the hut, John put the jug down just outside the door and stretched. He poured out some water into his hands and splashed his face. He walked over to Peter and asked if he had seen lightning or heard singing. Peter looked up in the sky and then back at John quizzically. He cocked his head, thinking that John was not a person prone to seeing things that were not there. None of the men were acting as if anything was amiss, so John shrugged and walked into the hut.

As he entered the hut, he was overwhelmed with the most fragrant scent he had ever experienced. He looked around for the source of the perfume and saw Mary's empty mat.

He circled the small hut and noticed that his own mat was now unrolled. He was sure he had rolled it up before he left for the water. Then he saw the flowers. They were tiny, white, star-shaped blossoms, and they were the source of the overpowering scent. John gathered the flowers into his arms as he remembered Mary's message to him just a short time ago.

Tears of joy and sadness began to trickle down his face. He waited a few minutes alone in the hut to gather his emotions before going out to those now eating their breakfast around the fire. After he had composed himself, John carried the bundle of flowers and walked outside. Everyone looked up at him with questioning glances. The beautiful scent of the flowers reached them, and they stopped eating.

Peter and Luke stood up and walked over to John. "Where is our mother?" they asked with quaking voices. John croaked through his tears, "Our blessed mother is no longer here on this earth."

The other men gathered closer, as they sensed something important was happening. John took a deep breath and said strongly, "Our mother Mary promised to help all of us, her children, in times of distress. We only need to call on her for aid. She can now help us as we travel to foreign parts of the world. She can go anywhere and do anything the Father permits. Our blessed mother promised to always be our mother and the path to her son." All of the men bowed their heads in silent prayer.

John bowed his head, turned and went back into the hut. Peter, Luke, and Paul followed him. They hugged one another and sat in stunned silence.

Eventually, Peter spoke up. "We must continue to carry on the work of Christ. We must also share with others how much we loved our blessed mother. I plan to travel to Rome." Each man shared where he felt called to travel. Peter nodded his approval and then closed his eyes as he led a prayer for their courage and faith. They were all aware that they were facing persecution and hard times.

When Peter finished the prayer, John raised his head and looked around the hut. He waved his arm and said, "We must take care of all of this before we leave."

They rose together and walked over to the large chest in the corner. The lid creaked as John lifted it slowly. Luke moved the table closer as John took out the first bundle of white linen and handed it reverently to Peter. Peter began to unroll it but found it much longer than the table. Paul took one side and Luke took the other as they stretched it out from one end of the hut to the other.

There was a collective gasp as the men realized what they were holding. It was the burial cloth of their Savior. The image of his body was clearly imprinted on the cloth. Every wound from the lash, the nails, even the thorn marks from his head were evident. Peter touched it reverently. Then he indicated to the men to roll it back up. Paul held it out to Peter, but Peter refused to take it. "Paul, you must take this with you on your journeys. It will help to convert many people." Paul touched it to his chest and could not speak. Then he put it into a large cloth sack he had slung over his body and buried it deep beneath his other possessions.

Peter, lifting the blood-stained robe of Jesus, said, "I will take this as a reminder of my sin. He was wearing this robe as I denied him." At this, they all shed a new tear. Peter laid the robe reverently on the table and nodded to John.

The next bundle John pulled out was large. As he unwrapped the package, he found two paintings Luke had done years ago. One was of Mary and the other was of Jesus as Mary had described him to Luke. John said, "Luke, these are remarkable. How did you capture Jesus' loving eyes so well?"

Luke replied, "Our mother described the Savior in great detail. It was not difficult."

John said, "Luke, you should take these with you and paint more so that others can love them as we do." Luke nodded wordlessly and put the pictures by the door.

John took out the veil of Seraphia that they had all seen last night. "Peter, who should take this?"

Peter had taken out a large rag from his pocket and was blowing his nose and wiping his face. He was overcome with grief and sadness. Then he said, "I think you should take this, John." They all nodded in agreement as John tucked it into his shirt.

At the very bottom of the chest, John found a small bundle he had not noticed before. When he unrolled it on the table, several thorns tumbled out. Some were as large as a man's thumb, and some were very tiny pieces of broken thorns.

John said, "After we had taken Jesus' body from the cross, we found Mary on the ground. She raised her arms to hold him one last time. I hesitated, as the body was so bloody and unrecognizable as the man we had all once known, but she was insistent. The other men helped me to lay his head in the crook of her arm and his chest across her lap. She stroked his matted hair, sticky with dried blood. As she did this, the thorns pricked her fingers. She began taking the thorns out, one by one. One of the men there, someone I don't know, sunk to the ground and began helping her. Many of the thorns were buried so deeply into his skull that they could only break them off. Mary and the man placed them in a little pile on a nearby stone. As we lifted his body and carried it to the stone outside the tomb for washing, Mary stood up and put the thorns into her pocket."

Peter suggested that each man outside, and the believers in town, should receive a thorn to remind them of Jesus' suffering. They all nodded and Peter put the thorns back into the bundle on the table.

John, thinking of the Christians in Ephesus, called out to Barnabas. He came into the hut immediately, his face still streaked with tears. John asked him to go into town and request that all of Mary's friends return to her hut as soon as possible. Before turning to leave, Barnabas looked at the open chest and the bundles on table and surmised what the men were about. He hesitated and then said through sobs, "May I have Mary's comb?" They looked at his bushy head and laughed for the first time that morning. "Of course, you may have it," John said as he searched in the bottom of the chest. "I'm sure our mother would be pleased." John handed the comb to Barnabas. He kissed it and headed down the hill immediately.

Next, John pulled out Jesus' chalice and handed it to Peter. Peter bowed low, took it, and kissed it. No one said a word. He placed it on the table and folded his hands.

They went back outside and waited for the Christians from Ephesus to arrive. They ate a bit of fruit and bread and shared with the men what they had decided to do with the relics.

When the people arrived, the few coins and extra clothing left in the chest were divided among those who needed them.

Now the chest was empty. Luke recalled how much Mary had loved this chest that Joseph had made for her. He turned to Peter, "May we offer this chest to Amos' family? I know little Ruth will honor it all of her life." Peter turned to John, and John nodded in ascent.

The other items in the hut—baskets, mats, blankets, goblets, bowls, and jugs—were divided among the followers from Ephesus.

And that was all there was. The home was emptied within a few hours, each person taking a precious reminder of their beloved mother.

Peter handed each one standing outside the hut a thorn that had pierced the head of Jesus.

Then he called them all into a close circle for a final prayer. "Bring all of your joys and sorrows, all of your hopes and despair, all that you are and lay it down at the feet of Jesus. Surrender all to him! He is your greatest friend and advocate. Only he can stand before the throne of the Father and plead for you. His blood was shed so that he could obtain that purpose and privilege. But never forget our blessed mother, who loves us with a love that surpasses all understanding. She gathers us beneath her mantle if we only ask. She can protect us from the snares of Satan. Never forget her. Never cease praying. Now, go in peace to love and serve the Lord."